AFTER THE GODS FELL SILENT

PARUL MATHUR

INDIA • SINGAPORE • MALAYSIA

ISBN
Paperback 979-8-89929-384-9
Hardcase 979-8-89984-552-9

Dedicated

to

Ravi & Vedaant

Contents

Prologue

As children, we heard the stories—

from grandparents at dusk, from parents during festivals, from books with fading pages, from movies glowing on old screens. Stories of four yugas, four great ages of time.

Satyug, when the Gods walked freely—Brahma created, Vishnu preserved, and Shiva transformed. The Devas ruled the heavens, and dharma flowed like an unbroken river.

Treta Yug, when Shri Ram, Maa Sita, and Shri Hanuman upheld righteousness in a world teetering on the edge of darkness.

Dwapar Yug, when Shri Krishna played his flute, spoke the Gita, and watched the great war unfold—where love, politics, and destiny danced their final dance.

And then came Kalyug—the age of confusion, corrosion, and forgetting. The age we live in.

We were told that one day, when things fall too far apart, Kalki would arrive. The final avatar. The restorer. The one who would end Kalyug and start the cycle anew.

But... Can you imagine the moment just before that happens?

When Kalyug is ending—

but Kalki has not yet come?

When the Gods have withdrawn,

but the new light hasn't yet risen?

A time suspended.

A world in between.

A silence stretched across sky and soul.

No thunder in the heavens.

No avatars in the palace.

Just… stillness.

This book was born in that stillness.

A stillness heavy with unanswered prayers.

With temples echoing only the footsteps of the faithful.

With questions that rise like smoke and dissolve into nothingness.

What happens when the Gods fall silent? When there are no more divine interventions, no more voices from the sky, no more miracles to hold on to?

What happens to faith when there is no one left to answer it?

This book is not a mythological retelling. It is a reflection of what comes after. After the leelas are done. After the epics are closed. After the conch has been blown… and faded.

This is a book about the ones left behind— The sages who search the silence.

The queens who carry memory like a wound.

The seekers who ask, not to rebel—but to remember.

And maybe, dear reader, you are one of them. One of us.

Still walking.

Still waiting.

Still believing…

After the gods fell silent.

And if you've ever looked up at the sky and whispered, 'Are you still there?' — this book is for you.

Preface

There are moments in life when the world grows quiet—not outside, but within. When the noise of certainty fades, and you find yourself sitting with questions you can no longer push away.

That's where I found myself—not as a writer, not even as a seeker—but as a human being trying to make sense of a world that felt both too full and strangely hollow. I kept turning to the **Bhagavad Gita** like one returns to a childhood home. Not always expecting answers, but hoping for something familiar, something grounding. And for a long time, that was enough. A verse here, a truth there. Just enough to keep going.

But slowly, a different kind of question began to grow inside me—not loud, but insistent. What if the age we live in—this complex, beautiful, broken age—isn't just **Kalyug**, but a quiet turning point? What if the gods we keep waiting for… are no longer coming?

It wasn't a loss of faith. It was something else. A shift. A sense that maybe we are not abandoned, but trusted. That maybe, for the first time, we are being asked to walk without being carried.

And that's how this story began—not with a plot, not with an idea, but with that simple, humbling thought:

What if the silence of the Gods is not their absence—but their invitation?

An invitation to choose. To act. To shape this world not through divine command, but through human courage.

After the God Fell Silent is not mythology.

It isn't fantasy.

It's simply a reflection—of a world learning to walk again.

A world no longer waiting for miracles, but trying—quietly, imperfectly—to become one.

If you've ever looked up and heard nothing...

If you've ever asked a question that came back as silence...

If you've ever wondered whether anyone is still listening… this book is for you.

It was never meant to tell a tale.

It was meant to ask a question.

And maybe, if we listen closely, we'll hear the answer in our own actions.

Thank you for walking this journey with me.

Thank you for choosing to read.

Thank you for choosing.

From my heart to yours,

Parul Mathur

About the Author

Parul Mathur is, above all else, someone who listens—with her heart, her words, and her silences. A storyteller by soul, a seeker by nature, and a mentor by choice, she has spent over two decades walking alongside people in their moments of doubt, transformation, and quiet rediscovery.

Her professional journey in Human Resources has earned her widespread recognition. She has been featured twice among Forbes India's Top 100 Great People Managers, 40 Under 40 HR Leaders awarded CHRO of the Year, named among India's Top 100 Women Leaders, and honoured as HR Leader by the Economic Times and HR Leader of the Year by HR Success Talk. But if you ask her what she values most, she won't mention titles. She'll speak of people—of real stories, difficult conversations, small breakthroughs, and the courage it takes to try again.

Her first book, *Those 30 Seconds*, received immense love for its simplicity, soul, and sincerity. Inspired by the timeless wisdom of the **Bhagavad Gita**, it invited readers into the sacred weight of a single moment—a space between reaction and reflection, where transformation quietly waits.

This book, *After the God Fell Silent*, is not a continuation, but a deepening. It emerges from questions that live beneath the surface—of faith, of silence, of what it means to choose when no divine voice is left to guide you. It is, in many ways, a quiet tribute to the strength we carry and the truths we must find for ourselves.

Parul holds academic degrees from Delhi University, IMT Ghaziabad, and XLRI Jamshedpur, and is currently pursuing her Ph.D. from Golden Gate University, USA. But her truest insights have come not from institutions, but from lived experience—through ancient texts, tender doubts, and the quiet bravery of simply continuing.

She does not write to impress.

She writes to be felt.

She writes to learn, and through learning, she hopes to share—gently, honestly, and without claiming to know it all.

A strong believer in the power of reflection, compassion, and conscious evolution, her personal motto remains simple:

Keep learning. Always.

She does not write to lead.

She writes to walk beside you—

quietly, sincerely, without knowing all the answers.

If her words feel like a pause, a breath,

or a moment where you remember you're not alone —
then she has written enough.

From her heart to yours,

Parul Mathur

Acknowledgement

Some books begin with an idea.

This one began with a feeling—quiet, persistent, and impossible to ignore.

To everyone who gave me space to think, to feel, to fall silent, and to begin again—thank you. Writing this book asked more of me than I expected, and your presence—just being there—mattered more than you know.

To the voices that shaped me over the years—through scriptures, conversations, and life itself—thank you for reminding me that faith isn't handed down. It's discovered. Often slowly, painfully, and with trembling hands.

To my readers—your love for my first book, Those 30 Seconds, became the bridge to this one. You held my words with such tenderness, and your responses gave me more courage than I had when I began. That book was born from a moment; this one from a silence. And yet, you met both with open hearts. For that, I am deeply grateful.

To my husband, **Ravi**—you are my support system, my safe place, and the voice that grounds me when my own feels faint. You have walked beside me without needing to understand every word—just trusting that they mattered. Thank you for holding steady when I doubted, for encouraging me when I paused, and for loving me with a quiet strength that gave this book its spine. Nothing I create stands alone—it stands because you never let me fall.

To my son, **Vedaant**—you are my life, my treasure, my compass. Your wonder, your questions, your clarity, and your kindness have shaped how I see the world. You are not just part of my reason to write—you are the reason I believe in the world I am writing toward. If this book carries any truth, it is because of what you continue to teach me, simply by being you.

To those who have stood beside me—not to lead, not to rescue, but just to stay—thank you. Your quiet presence became the space where this book could finally breathe.

And to anyone who has ever looked at the silence above and wondered if it still holds meaning—this book is for you.

With all my heart,

Parul Mathur

Chapter 1

The Dawn of Karma Yug

A sky burdened with despair stretched endlessly, its ashen veil swallowing the world below. The air reeked of decay, a putrid mix of rotting earth and burnt remnants of a world that once thrived. Blackened mud stretched across the land, cracked and lifeless, where rivers once flowed. Misshapen cacti loomed, eerie guardians of a world long abandoned. A heavy silence choked the air, broken only by distant, haunting howls of untamed creatures.

Once familiar creatures had morphed into terrifying shadows of their past selves. Rats, now the size of large dogs, scuttled across the land, their beady eyes gleaming in the dim light. Once-playful dogs, now grotesque and swollen, prowled with guttural howls, hunting all in their path. Horses, their bodies bloated and monstrous, trotted through the desolate plains with the weight of ancient memories. They were no longer the majestic creatures of old but towering behemoths, their hooves thundering as they stomped across the earth. And then, there were the elephants—once noble and revered, now beasts the size of entire cities, with tusks that scraped the sky, their very presence a reminder of the world's unnatural decay.

Once-proud cities had crumbled into heaps of rubble, their towering monuments now mere shadows of lost glory. Streets were buried under layers of blackened dust, and skeletal remains lay strewn across the ruins—silent witnesses to an era of greed and destruction. Even the trees, twisted and gnarled, bore no leaves, only jagged thorns that pierced the air like remnants of a long-forgotten agony. The ground beneath was slick with a mixture of mud and ash, the very soil that once nurtured life now an inhospitable wasteland.

Humans, if they could still be called that, had shrunk to the size of dwarfs—frail, hunched, and barely recognizable as the grand beings they once were. Their hollow eyes gazed up at the heavens, waiting. Belief clung to them like the ragged clothes barely covering their emaciated forms. They whispered among themselves, their feeble voices laced with desperation. Their bodies, shivering in the cold embrace of endless twilight, bore the marks of generations lost in darkness.

"Satya Yuga will come," they murmured. "The gods will save us. We will ascend with divine powers."

A group of survivors huddled in a ruined temple, their emaciated bodies wrapped in tattered robes. Their faces were gaunt, their eyes hollow with exhaustion, yet there was an arrogance in their voices, a belief that they alone were the chosen ones, destined to enter the Satya Yuga.

"We are the survivors," one of them declared, standing taller than the rest despite his frail form. "Our karmas were pure. The gods spared us. We will be the ones to ascend, to join the gods in Satya Yuga."

His voice was filled with a strange superiority, an arrogance that clung to him like a heavy cloak. The others nodded in agreement, their eyes filled with a mixture of pride and defiance.

"While the others perished, we endured," another survivor added, his chest puffed out, his voice filled with conviction. "We are the chosen few."

"The gods have spared us for a reason," a woman, her hands clutching a broken idol, sneered. "We are better than the rest. The dead do not matter. We are the worthy ones."

A younger man, his eyes burning with the fire of defiance, shook his head. *"You are fools. Do you not see? We are waiting for Satya Yuga to come. We are the ones who have been spared! We will rise! We are better than the rest!"*

But even as he spoke, doubt began to creep into his voice. The land was silent, its stillness a harsh reminder that the gods had not answered. There was no salvation. No divine intervention. The sky remained gray, the earth remained barren, and their prayers echoed into the void.

An elder, his bones creaking with age, looked at the group with sorrowful eyes. *"You believe you are better, that you are the chosen ones. But tell me, where are the gods? Why does Satya Yuga not come? Why do we remain here, in this world of rot and decay?"*

A long silence followed. The arrogance in their voices faltered, replaced by a whisper of fear.

"What if the gods have abandoned us?" the elder whispered, his voice filled with the weight of realization. *"What if we are not chosen after all? What if we are the ones left behind, forgotten?"*

The group shifted uncomfortably, the certainty in their voices now wavering.

"No," the young man retorted, his voice sharp, *"the cycle must turn! Satya Yuga will come. The gods will save us!"*

A man in tattered robes, his body gaunt and weak, laughed bitterly. *"Save us? The gods have saved no one. We were left behind, abandoned to live in this hellish world. There is no salvation."*

Another survivor, his voice trembling with bitterness, added, *"If we were chosen, why do we suffer? Where is our reward? The heavens are cold to our pleas, and we are left to rot."*

The woman clutching the broken idol laughed harshly, her face twisted with arrogance. *"The gods have saved us. Do not speak of this nonsense. We are the last remnants of the worthy."*

The elder shook his head, his eyes heavy with sorrow. *"Saved? No. We were merely left behind. And that is what frightens me the most."* His voice quivered with the finality of truth, as though the weight of a forgotten world pressed down on him.

Above them, the sky remained unchanged—a blank slate of ash, a reminder that there was no divine presence, no future to look forward to. Only the earth remained, broken, decayed, and suffocating under the weight of its own destruction.

Above the ruined earth, the celestial realm vibrated with an energy far heavier than the gods had ever known. The gods of the celestial court gathered in the Sabha Mandala, their golden thrones reflecting the gravity of the moment. Their luminous forms shimmered in the vast expanse of the heavens, but even the ethereal light could not erase the weight of their impending decision. The air crackled with energy, as though the very cosmos held its breath.

At the center, the divine Brahma, his form shifting like the tides of time, gazed upon the ruined world below. His voices echoed with sorrow, frustration, and a hint of fury.

Brahma, the Creator, stood first, his four faces betraying his anger and disappointment. *"And yet, look at what we have created. Look at them!"* With a sweeping gesture, his hand stretched toward the mortal realm below. The air of frustration in his voice was palpable as his gaze cut through the charred remnants of Kalyug. *"They have twisted everything—our gifts, our blessings—into poison. They squandered their time, and now we are left to pick up the pieces."* His eyes smoldered with fury. *"What is Satya Yuga to them? A new stage to repeat their sins with impunity?"*

The divine court fell silent, as Brahma's words echoed across the chamber. The air became thick with tension, the gods themselves questioning the futility of Satya Yuga.

Vishnu, ever the voice of reason and balance, leaned forward, his serene face unshaken by Brahma's fury. *"If we continue this endless cycle, we condemn them to repeat their mistakes, to fall into the same traps of greed and pride. Satya Yuga will not purify them; it will only set the stage for their inevitable corruption."* His words were calm, but each syllable carried the weight of a thousand years of wisdom. *"We must sever the chain. To preserve the balance of existence, to protect the future of creation, we must choose a new path."*

"I understand your frustration, Brahma, but the cycle must end. If we give them another Satya Yuga, it will only perpetuate this endless loop of creation, corruption, and destruction. They need to learn on their own, without divine intervention. We cannot hold their hands any longer. We have provided them with the path, and they have twisted it. A new age must rise. But it cannot be one of perfect righteousness as in Satya Yuga. They must learn from their choices. They must know the true weight of their actions. This is why Karma Yug must be."

But Indra, ever the protector of order, could not contain his disbelief. His brow furrowed, his voice thick with frustration.

"Karma Yug? What is this nonsense?" Indra stood, his lightning-sculpted form crackling with irritation. *"If we abandon the cycle altogether, what will become of the world? Without Satya Yuga, there is nothing but chaos! You propose Karma Yug—an age where the consequences of actions govern everything—but what of dharma? What of the moral compass that guides mankind? Without dharma, how will they know right from wrong? How will they not descend into anarchy?"*

Varuna, the god of oceans, his presence as vast as the seas themselves, nodded in agreement, his voice like a rising tide.

"If there is no Yuga, then there is no order. The seas themselves rise and fall with time, with rhythm, with purpose. How can mortals find their way without a divine code? Karma Yug may punish the wicked, but what of the good? Without dharma, there is no balance, no guidance. It is too impartial! They will twist it to suit their own ends."

Chandra Dev, the moon god, a figure of serenity in the cosmic turmoil, added softly but pointedly, *"Without dharma, how will they know the meaning of selfless devotion? How can the light of goodness shine if there is no guiding principle, no righteousness to follow?"*

Ganga Maa, with her flowing, ever-present grace, spoke next, her voice tinged with the sorrow of the sacred rivers that once flowed with clarity and purity. *"In every age, the river of dharma has flowed to guide them. But if you remove dharma, what will guide them? Karma may dictate actions, but what will give them purpose? Without dharma, they are like a river without a bank—lost, directionless."*

Shiva, the great destroyer, stood silently through the growing discord, the weight of the decision pressing upon his heart like the weight of mountains. His voice, when it finally broke the silence, resonated with the force of cosmic truth.

"Dharma has become corrupted," Shiva said, his words heavy with finality. *"The mortals have twisted it for their own gains,*

using it as a shield for their selfishness. They no longer honor it as they once did. To return to Dharma Yug would be to reward them for their blindness, their failure to learn. They will abuse dharma again, just as they have done with every cycle before."

His eyes flared with a divine fire as he continued, *"I say this not out of malice, but out of necessity. Karma alone is incorruptible. It is the truth of the universe. It does not bend to the will of the powerful or the manipulative. Only through Karma Yug will they learn the consequences of their actions. There is no other way. They must face the weight of their choices directly, without relying on us to clean up their mess."*

Vishnu, whose calm exterior had begun to betray the depths of his inner turmoil, added, *"Dharma Yug has had its time. Mortals have come to expect righteousness to be handed to them, rather than earned. They have grown complacent, assuming that dharma will always be their crutch. But this has led them astray. Now they must walk without it. Karma will be their teacher. The age of divine guidance is over. They must take responsibility for themselves."*

Indra's fury boiled over, his voice rising like a tempest. *"But what of the devoted? What of those who have strived for righteousness all their lives? You will throw them into the same chaos as the wicked? How will they know what is truly right?"*

Brahma responded, his voice sharp and clear. *"This is the very point, Indra. Those who have strived for righteousness will rise above. They will not falter in the face of Karma Yug. But those who have hidden behind dharma, those who have used it for their own purposes, will fall. This is the only way. They will be forced to face* the consequences of their actions. Dharma alone cannot guide them anymore. Karma will reveal the truth."

Brahma sighed deeply, his gaze turning toward the heavens, where the constellations shimmered faintly. "Dharma was the foundation, yes. But it has been corrupted beyond recognition. The mortals no longer respect it; they twist it to suit their own desires. They have become so blinded by their own greed that they no longer see the truth. They use Dharma as a tool for their ambitions, as a means to justify their cruelty and pride."

Shiva, who had been silent until now, opened his eyes slowly, his gaze burning like fire. "They have turned Dharma into a weapon. A tool for their own self-interest. I have watched them, again and again, twist it to their advantage. They no longer honor it; they use it as a shield against their own karma." His voice grew louder, his words heavy with finality. "If we grant them another Dharma Yug, they will only desecrate it. They must stand without crutches. They must learn the true meaning of their actions, without the divine interference. Karma Yug will teach them that."

The silence in the divine court deepened as the gods pondered Shiva's words. Finally, Brahma spoke, his voice heavy with the decision that had been made. "Karma Yug will rise. It will not ask them to follow Dharma blindly. It will teach them the true weight of their actions, the consequences of their choices. Only then will they understand the essence of righteousness. Only then will they be worthy of the divine guidance they once took for granted."

The entire court fell silent. Even Agni, the fire god, who had long held the flame of passion in his heart, had no words. There was no argument left. Only the undeniable force of fate remained.

"I see now," Indra murmured, his voice heavy with doubt. *"This is the path we must take, then. A gamble unlike any before. We break the cycle. We step aside. Let them find their own way."*

And so it was decided. The divine decree echoed throughout the celestial realm, reverberating across the vast expanse of time and space, sealing the fate of mortals below.

There would be no Satya Yuga. There would be no Dharma Yug. Only Karma Yug remained—the age where each soul would bear the weight of its own actions, forging its own destiny, for better or worse. The gods had spoken. And so, a new age began.

As the decree was made, the gods knew the cosmos would be forever changed. The mortal world would no longer be guided by the cycles of Dharma. Instead, they would be forced to face the raw consequences of their choices, their actions shaping their destinies.

As the three supreme gods stood together, the enormity of their collective realization settled over them like a heavy cloud. Kalyug, though full of turmoil and destruction, had been the teacher, and they had learned far more than they could have imagined. They had witnessed humanity at its lowest, but they had also glimpsed what could be if humanity was granted the freedom to choose, to learn, and to rise.

Vishnu, with his serene and contemplative gaze, broke the silence once again. *"In Kalyug, we saw the blindness of humanity—how, in the pursuit of righteousness, they became rigid and detached from the essence of life itself. They clung to duty and tradition, not out of understanding, but out of fear and obligation. People lost sight of the inner self. They allowed the forces of the world to shape them, rather than recognizing their own ability to shape their fate through their actions. Kalyug showed us that when people forget the connection between their choices and their consequences, they fall into darkness. The imbalance created by this ignorance brought forth destruction."*

He paused, his words lingering in the air like a silent warning. *"We cannot return to that, for if we did, we would be condemning humanity to a life of blind obedience and suffering. We must give them the power to choose—to shape their own destiny. That is the greatest lesson of Kalyug: that humanity must learn to embrace their own strength, their own karma."*

Brahma nodded in agreement, his face a canvas of ancient wisdom. *"Yes, Vishnu. Kalyug was a time of great devastation, but it was also a time of awakening. We saw how the cycles of life and death became distorted. The people no longer understood the consequences of their actions because they were disconnected from their own essence. They turned to external forces—gods, fate, destiny—believing that these would guide them. But in doing so, they relinquished their own power. They became victims of their circumstances, trapped in the illusion that they were powerless."*

He let out a heavy sigh, the weight of the truth pressing upon him. *"This is the true lesson of Kalyug: power does not lie in external forces. Power lies in the choices we make. In Karma Yug, there will be no more excuses. Mankind will have to face their own reflections—no one will save them but themselves."*

Shiva's deep, resonant voice followed, his eyes glowing with the intensity of a truth that had long been hidden. *"Kalyug revealed a truth that shook even me. In the rush for power, for control, for survival, humanity became blind to the essence of their existence. The desire to possess, to dominate, to control—this hunger led them into a spiral of destruction. They lost sight of the most fundamental law of existence: everything is interconnected. Every action, every thought, every word has a consequence. In Kalyug, they believed they could escape the repercussions of their actions, that they could escape karma itself. But the truth, as we saw, is unavoidable."*

Shiva's gaze became sharper, filled with conviction. *"The realization here is simple, yet profound: in Kalyug, humanity ignored the very foundation of existence—karma. They chased external validation, power, and pleasure, without considering the effect of their choices on the world around them. This is why Karma Yug must begin. Humanity must understand that they are the architects of their own fate. They must learn to embrace karma, not as a force of punishment, but as a force of growth, of learning, and of transformation."*

For a long moment, silence filled the heavens as the gods reflected on the weight of their shared lessons. The truth of Kalyug was undeniable, and the purpose of Karma Yug became even clearer.

Vishnu, Brahma, and Shiva all turned their gazes toward the earth below, their eyes filled with a renewed sense of purpose.

Vishnu spoke again, his voice filled with quiet strength. *"In Karma Yug, there will be no easy answers, no simple solutions. The world will be shaped by the choices of each individual, and every action will carry weight. Mankind will no longer be passive recipients of fate. They will be the creators of their own destiny. And this is why we have chosen the Seven Sages to guide them. These sages will embody the wisdom of karma, showing humanity that their path is not predetermined but forged through their own choices."*

Brahma's voice followed, filled with the certainty of creation itself. *"Karma Yug is not about divine intervention. It is about self-realization. Each individual must come to understand that they are not mere players in a grand game. They are the masters of their own fate. The sages will not provide answers—they will provide the tools to discover the answers within. They will not be heroes—they will be teachers. And through their teachings, humanity will learn the greatest lesson of all: that the key to life lies within themselves, within their own actions."*

Shiva's voice, as always, was the most potent. *"Karma is the ultimate teacher. It will show no mercy, but it will also show no bias. The actions of the individual will determine their destiny. There will be no gods to intercede, no divine forces to step in and correct the wrongs. In this age, mankind will be free—not from suffering, but from the illusion that they are helpless. They will learn that their choices matter, that their actions have consequences, and that their very existence is a reflection of their own karma."*

The sky above the ruined earth grew darker as the winds of change began to stir. And somewhere, in the distant reaches of the universe, the seeds of Karma Yug were sown. The dawn of a new era was upon them, an era where mortals would no longer wait for divine intervention. They would learn, through their own deeds, what it meant to be truly righteous.

As the gods stood in unison, their words echoing across the universe, they understood the magnitude of the decision they had made. Karma Yug would be a time of profound transformation. It would not be easy, and it would not be merciful. But it would be real. Humanity would finally be forced to face the consequences of their actions, and in doing so, they would rediscover their true strength.

The Fall of Human Integrity

Vishnu: *"In Kalyug, humans lost their sense of integrity. Leaders who should have upheld dharma became self-serving, driven by personal desires rather than the welfare of their people. This led to the rise of corruption, deceit, and manipulation. Instead of nurturing their communities, they tore them apart for their own gain. If they had understood the power of their actions—karma— and realized that a ruler's true strength lies in justice, honesty, and service, they could have avoided the collapse of trust that ensued."*

Lesson for Karma Yug: In Karma Yug, the people will understand that their integrity is the foundation of their power. Leaders and individuals alike will know that true power comes from selfless actions, not from manipulating others.

The Disregard for Nature

Shiva: *"Kalyug also saw the most egregious disregard for nature and the balance of the earth. Humans exploited resources without respect, ravaging the planet for short-term gain. In their greed, they forgot that the Earth is not a resource to be exhausted, but a living entity that sustains all life. If only they had recognized the importance of balance in their karma, they would have known that when they harm nature, they harm themselves in the process. A world cannot survive when it is at war with itself."*

Lesson for Karma Yug: In Karma Yug, humans will no longer be able to ignore the consequences of their actions against the earth. They will realize that the health of nature is inseparable from their own survival, and the duty to protect it will be seen as an act of cosmic responsibility.

The Ignorance of True Wisdom

Brahma: *"Perhaps the greatest failing of Kalyug was the loss of true wisdom. Knowledge became fragmented, divided into isolated fields, and spiritual wisdom was overshadowed by material pursuits. Mankind sought knowledge, but they did not seek wisdom. Many turned to false doctrines, pretending to know the truth, while abandoning the deep, unchanging truths of the universe. If they had only understood that wisdom lies in the realization of one's actions—karma—on a spiritual and practical level, they could have avoided the fragmentation of knowledge and the chaos that followed."*

Lesson for Karma Yug: In Karma Yug, mankind will rediscover the connection between knowledge and wisdom. They will see that true wisdom is understanding the impact of one's actions on the world and acting in harmony with the universal laws of karma.

Kalyug had been a time of darkness, but it had given them the greatest gift—the gift of understanding. And now, with the dawn of Karma Yug, the gods knew that humanity would be given the greatest opportunity of all: the opportunity to choose.

The Seven Sages would lead the way, and through their guidance, mankind would walk the difficult but ultimately redemptive path of self-discovery, growth, and transformation.

As the gods convened in the celestial court, the weight of their decision pressed upon their shoulders like the very fabric of time itself. The assembly was hushed, the divine voices echoing in the vast space, their words rippling through the cosmic ether. The question of the Seven Sages lingered, an unresolved tension in the air.

Varuna, the god of oceans, rose once more, his voice rippling like the waves of the deep. *"Seven?"* His gaze swept across the divine council. *"Why not three? Or five? Seven seems... excessive. Wouldn't fewer be more focused, more concentrated in their purpose?"*

A murmur of agreement rippled through the court, but Brahma, the Creator, remained unfazed. He leaned forward, his voice steady, yet carrying the weight of infinite creation. *"Varuna, the number seven is not arbitrary. It is the number of completeness, the number of balance. Seven is the perfect number, the foundation of the universe itself. In every realm, in every cycle, seven is the key to harmony."*

He paused, allowing the significance of his words to sink in. *"Seven is not too much; it is precisely what is needed to bring balance to the broken world. Each sage must embody a unique aspect of karma. Justice, duty, sacrifice, wisdom, compassion, resilience, and truth—these are the virtues that will guide mankind, and each sage will serve as a living example of one of these qualities."*

Indra, ever the skeptic, folded his arms and raised an eyebrow. *"But why must there be so many? Why not distill it into fewer sages, each embodying multiple virtues? Three sages should be enough to carry the weight of Karma Yug."*

Brahma's gaze was unwavering, his four faces all observing the divine assembly. *"Indra, do you not see? Three sages cannot encompass the full spectrum of karma. It is too narrow, too limited. Mankind has faltered because they have been given too little to guide them. They have focused only on a single path—the path of devotion, or the path of dharma, or the path of knowledge. But Karma Yug is different. It requires a deeper understanding of the universe—an understanding of how each action, no matter how small, ripples outward to create consequences."*

Vishnu, ever the mediator, spoke next, his voice soft yet carrying a depth of wisdom. *"Think of the seven notes in a musical scale, Varuna. Alone, each note may be beautiful, but it is only together, in harmony, that they create the symphony of existence. The Seven Sages will guide mankind, not in isolation, but in balance. Without one, the others would falter, and the teachings would become incomplete."*

Varuna's brow furrowed as he absorbed the weight of Brahma's words. *"But still, why not five? Or two? Seven seems... too much. Could we not achieve the same with a smaller number?"*

Shiva, who had remained silent until now, opened his eyes, his voice low and rumbling like distant thunder. *"Varuna, the very essence of Karma Yug is not in simplicity but in complexity. Each of the Seven Sages represents a different facet of karma. To ask for fewer would be to dilute the teachings. Karma is not a single, simple principle—it is a web, a network of interconnected actions and consequences. Each sage will embody one of these principles, and through their lives, mortals will come to understand the vastness of their choices."*

His gaze swept over the assembly, his eyes burning with divine fire. *"Just as the cosmos is vast and infinite, so too must be the teachings of Karma Yug. Three sages would not be enough to encompass the entirety of this new age. Karma is not simply about justice or duty—it is about the intertwining of all these virtues. And that, Varuna, is why there must be seven."*

Brahma's gaze deepened, his expression carrying the weight of untold ages. He was the Creator, the architect of worlds, and yet in this moment, he spoke not with the detachment of a deity, but with a quiet reverence for the cosmic law that governed all things. The question had been asked—why seven? And this time, his answer would not be a simple declaration, but an unveiling of the very fabric of the universe.

"Seven," Brahma began, his voice reverberating through the celestial halls, *"is not merely a number. It is the key to the rhythm of existence itself. It is the first echo in the vast emptiness, the shape of time itself."*

The gods fell silent, drawn into his words, sensing that something deeper was being revealed. Vishnu, always attuned to the pulse of the universe, leaned forward, his eyes reflecting the infinite.

Brahma continued, his tone now carrying the weight of infinite cycles. *"Seven is not a creation of the gods, but the very essence of creation itself. It is the first number that reaches beyond the singular, beyond the dual. One is unity; two is duality. But three, three births the first complexity—three creates a foundation, but it is only with four that we find the square of balance, the four corners of the universe. But it is seven that unlocks the mystery of life. Seven is not just balance; it is the law of the cosmos, the divine symmetry that holds all things in place."*

He raised his hand as if to trace the unseen lines of the universe, the air around him shimmering with the threads of destiny. *"Consider this—seven is the first number that encompasses all possibilities. The seven colors of the rainbow are not just a visual spectacle—they represent the full spectrum of reality. Seven notes form the very foundation of harmony. Seven celestial bodies mark the passage of time, the cycle of creation and destruction. Seven is not just a number—it is a threshold, the point where the finite meets the infinite."*

The gods exchanged knowing glances, but it was Narad who spoke next, his voice a deep resonance that seemed to vibrate through the core of creation. *"But what makes seven the true number? Why not five, or eleven, or any other combination of cosmic forces?"*

Brahma turned to him, his eyes shining with the ancient knowledge. *"Because seven is the first number where all things come together in harmony. It is the number of completion, but also the number of the journey. When you reach seven, you are at the point of wholeness, but you have also transcended. You see, to understand karma, you must first understand the full spectrum of existence—the balance between creation and destruction, the dance between light and shadow, the flow between desire and restraint. Seven is the number that encompasses all of this."*

He paused, his eyes locking with the divine assembly. *"The Seven Sages are not mere servants of fate—they are the embodiments of this cosmic law. Each sage represents a different facet of karma, but together, they are the complete wheel. Without one, the others would falter, and without them all, the world would collapse into chaos. Seven represents the harmony between individual choice and universal law, between action and consequence, between the mortal and the divine."*

Indra, his skepticism slowly fading, asked, *"But how can seven embody all of this? What is the true mystery behind the number?"*

Brahma smiled, his expression both enigmatic and knowing. *"Seven is the secret of the universe. It is the balance between the manifested and the unmanifested. It is the first number that reaches into the void and brings forth existence. In the first creation, there was the One—the singular, the undifferentiated. But the One divided into two, and from that duality arose the need for three—the first dynamic. Four became the foundation, and five the expansion of that foundation. But it is seven that completes the cycle. Seven is the final key. It represents the intersection of all forces—the forces of creation, preservation, destruction, and the cycles that bind them."*

He stepped forward, his voice growing more intense. *"When you understand the mystery of seven, you understand the very nature of fate itself. The Seven Sages will not only embody the principles of karma—they will also be the carriers of this secret. Each one will be the living manifestation of one of the seven fundamental forces of existence, and together, they will show mankind the path to enlightenment. They will teach them that karma is not a simple matter of reward and punishment—it is the essence of existence itself. It is the pulse of life."*

Shiva, his eyes glowing with understanding, nodded slowly. *"And the sages will walk the earth, not as gods, but as embodiments of this law. They will guide mankind not through divine miracles, but by the force of their own understanding of the universe's deepest secrets."*

"Yes," Brahma said, his voice growing softer, but filled with a deep resonance. *"They will not be teachers in the traditional sense. They will not offer miracles or blessings. They will show mankind that their every action, no matter how small, is part of a much greater cycle. A cycle that they must navigate themselves. Karma is not a burden—it is a freedom. And it is through understanding the sevenfold nature of existence that mankind will be able to truly shape their own fate."*

The other gods were silent, each contemplating the weight of this decision. Vishnu, his voice serene yet filled with certainty, added, *"The number seven will also ensure that there is no overreliance on a single aspect of karma. If we had only one sage, they would become an idol, a figure to be worshipped, and mortals would once again miss the true lesson. But seven... seven will be seen as a diverse force, a living representation of the many facets of karma, and none will be able to elevate one above the others."*

Shiva's eyes narrowed, and he judged everyone's anxiety. He started asking on everyone's behalf, *"That is their purpose. They are not gods, nor are they mortals. They are the bridge between the two. They are the ones who will show mankind the path, not by wielding divine power, but by living with the consequences of their own choices. They will teach them that they, too, have the power to shape their destiny."*

Brahma nodded solemnly. *"We will not interfere. They will guide the mortals, but the path they choose will be theirs alone. No more gods coming down to save them. No more divine interventions. Karma will be the only guide, the only law.*

The gods sat in rapt silence, contemplating the gravity of what had been said. For in that moment, they understood that the Seven Sages were not just agents of the new age—they were the living manifestations of the cosmos itself. Each one would carry the burden of their own principle, but together, they would be the bridge to the future, the key to unlocking the potential of Karma Yug.

And with that, the first rays of Karma Yug began to shine, and the Seven Sages descended, bringing with them not the grace of divine intervention, but the wisdom of the cosmos itself. The age of Karma Yug had begun, and with it, a new chapter in the story of existence.

Indra, still unsure, finally spoke, his voice tinged with both resistance and acceptance. *"So, seven it will be. Seven sages, each representing a unique facet of karma. But can they truly stand alone? Can they guide the mortals without divine intervention?"*

A heavy silence fell upon the assembly as the gods absorbed the magnitude of their decision. Varuna, though still skeptical, nodded slowly. *"So, the Seven Sages will walk among mortals, guiding them not by divine miracle, but by example. Seven sages, each representing a different facet of karma. I see now why the number is necessary."*

Indra, too, seemed to accept the logic, though his skepticism remained. *"This will be a test unlike any we have ever seen. The balance of the cosmos rests on the success of this venture."*

Vishnu smiled softly. "The cosmos has always been in flux, Indra. It is time for the mortals to learn the greatest lesson of all—that their actions, and their karma, are their own to bear."

And so, with a single decree, the decision was made. Seven sages, neither divine nor mortal, would walk the earth, guiding mankind through the dawning age of Karma Yug. Each sage would represent a different aspect of karma—justice, duty, sacrifice, wisdom, compassion, resilience, and truth. Together, they would help rebuild a world torn asunder by the failures of the past, not with miracles, but with wisdom.

And with that, the first rays of Karma Yug began to shine upon the world below, and the Seven Sages began their descent, their presence igniting hope in the hearts of mankind. The age of Karma Yug had begun.

Vishnu's gaze swept across the assembly, a quiet assurance in his words. *"What we give them now is not the illusion of divine protection, nor the false comfort of guaranteed victory. We give them something far more powerful: the ability to create their own destiny. Karma Yug will be an age where their actions—every thought, every decision—will shape their fate. They will not be guided by the invisible strings of divine control, nor will they wait for saviors to rise. No. They will rise through the strength of their own hearts and minds. This, my fellow gods, is true hope: the ability for mortals to become their own creators of destiny, not dependent on us, but empowered by themselves."*

Shiva's voice broke the silence, strong yet tempered with deep understanding. *"In Kalyug, humanity was lost—drowned in their own vices and distractions. They sought external sources of power, believing that the gods could change their world. But Kalyug taught us that power, if not earned and understood by one's own will, only leads to destruction. Now, in Karma Yug, they will be forced to reckon with their actions. There will be no divine rescue. Only the consequences of their choices will guide them. It is not mercy we offer them; it is the greatest gift—freedom. The hope we hold out to them is the opportunity to rebuild themselves, from within. Each one, no matter how small, will have the power to change the course of their future through the purity of their karma."*

In this new age, no one would be saved by divine intervention. They would save themselves. And that, the gods knew, was the only way forward.

These words were not mere declarations; they carried the wisdom of a new age, one where hope was not a passive gift but an active, deliberate force in the hands of those who chose to embrace it. As the gods spoke, their unity resonated in the divine space, echoing a belief in the intrinsic strength of all beings, waiting to be awakened in the hearts of mankind.

And thus, with neither sword nor scripture, but with silence and divine consent, the old cycle ended. Satya, Treta, Dwapar, and Kalyug faded into memory. What rose was not a golden age, but a mirror held to mankind.

The Gods stepped back, and the Seven Sages stepped forward.

No more shall mortals wait for the sky to split open, for saviors to descend.

From this moment onward,

"The divine shall reside not above, but within."

This is Karma Yug:

Where every action is a prayer, Where every silence carries weight.

Where destiny is no longer given, but earned.

The wheel has turned, The gods have spoken.

The future now belongs to those who dare to choose.

From their hearts to yours, the age of Karma begins.

Whispers of Karma

"Let no star above deceive you,

No prophecy proclaim your fate.

The world no longer leans on gods,

But on choices we create.

No savior shall return in gold,

No chariot shall cleave the sky.

Your dharma walks beside your soul,

Your karma never dies.

The age of mirrored consequence

Now holds the sacred key.

To rise, to fall, to bloom, to burn—

Is yours eternally.

So tread with heart, and speak with truth,

Let silence bear your name.

For this is not a time of gods,

But of the human flame."

Chapter 2

The Chosen Seven

The heavens trembled as the cosmic assembly gathered, a surge of divine energy cascading across the universe like a mighty storm. In the infinite expanse above, three distinct radiances clashed and converged—the golden glow of Brahma's wisdom, serene yet all-encompassing, stretched across the void like the first light of dawn. Vishnu's steady blue radiance, the hue of a vast ocean, swirled with calm purpose, his presence as enduring as time itself. And the fierce red flames of Shiva's destruction ignited the sky in a wild tempest, crackling with primal force, as if ready to consume everything in its path.

These lights, each representing a fundamental aspect of existence—creation, preservation, and destruction—formed a celestial triad above the shattered earth. The world below, once teeming with life and vitality, lay in ruins. The earth was cracked, jagged fissures gaping open like the wounds of a dying creature, emitting a heat that scorched the very air. Smoldering remnants of the past age clung to the earth—great fires of molten metal and charred ruins that seemed to bleed ashen wind. The remnants of once-immense forests were now twisted, blackened skeletons of their former selves, and the heavens above wept with eternal storms, their grey skies heavy with sorrow.

Standing before the cosmic trinity, seven figures emerged from the chaos. Their forms were as distinct as their fates, each a being of immense power and wisdom, chosen for their unique qualities and strengths. They stood tall and firm on the cracked earth, despite the uncertainty in their hearts. Some stood with heads bowed in humility, others with a quiet defiance, yet all were cloaked in a shroud of doubt. Each sage had been summoned for this moment—the moment when the future of the universe would be forged, not through divine intervention, but through their very actions, choices, and karma.

These were the Seven Sages: Rudrayan, The Hammer of Justice—his broad shoulders and unyielding presence radiating authority, his heavy gaze steady like an unmovable mountain; Satyavrat, The Bearer of Truth—his eyes piercing with the clarity of an eternal flame, his form slender yet strong, unbroken by the weight of the harshest truths; Anirvan, The Flame of Courage—his figure burning with an inner light, his face unflinching as if nothing could quench the fire that fueled him; Vidyatman, The Keeper of Knowledge—his serene countenance reflecting an infinite ocean of wisdom, his mind an uncharted realm of insights and truths; Karunesh, The Vessel of Mercy—his aura exuding a deep, compassionate calm, his very presence a balm for the wounded world; Yuktashakti, The Weaver of Fate— her form wrapped in an ethereal glow, her hands weaving the threads of destiny itself, her mind a labyrinth of infinite possibilities; Nirvansh, The Master of Desire— his demeanor calm yet intense, his heart a storm of passions held in check, his very essence one of boundless will.

Despite their divine power and the wisdom bestowed upon them, there was an undeniable weight of uncertainty that hung in the air. Each of them knew the importance of their task, but no matter how powerful they were, they were not immune to doubt. The path ahead was unknown, and the challenge they faced was unlike anything they had ever encountered. They were not here to wield divine power over the mortal realm, but to guide it through a new age—a new age born of balance and karma, where neither gods nor mortals would hold absolute dominion, but rather, all would be equal before the law of karma.

As the Seven Sages stood before the cosmic trinity, the air crackled with anticipation. The gods had summoned them, but now, the gravity of their responsibility weighed heavily upon them.

Brahma, the Creator, with his four faces reflecting the myriad aspects of the universe—contemplation, foresight, wisdom, and fate—looked down upon them from above. His eyes glimmered with the profound depths of all creation, his presence an unspoken promise of guidance and wisdom. His deep, resonant voice filled the heavens, reverberating across time and space, as though the very cosmos itself listened to his every word.

"The world has fallen into ruin," Brahma began, *his voice echoing through the very fabric of existence. "Not by the wrath of gods, but by the folly of men. The age of divine intervention is over. You, the*

Seven Chosen, are the architects of Karma Yug. The time has come for the world to be shaped not by the hands of deities, but by the actions and consequences of those who walk upon it."

Each sage stood still, absorbing the weight of Brahma's words. They could feel their hearts sink beneath the immense gravity of their mission. This was not a task of conquest, nor of divine control—it was a challenge to reshape the very essence of existence itself.

"Your task is not to rule," Brahma continued, his gaze moving from one sage to the next. *"But to guide. Not to destroy, but to rebuild. You must shape the world through karma, not through power, but through purpose. The balance of the universe now rests in your hands. You must not only create a new age, but ensure that this age remains true to the fundamental principles of balance, righteousness, and justice."*

Each sage stood in contemplation, feeling the immense weight of what was being asked of them. The path was not one of glory or grandeur, but of discipline and sacrifice. Brahma's words rang in their minds like a clarion call, reminding them that their roles were not to act as gods, but as shepherds to the world.

"Before you embark on this journey, you must understand that this is no easy path," Brahma continued, his voice a quiet thunder that seemed to shake the very heavens. "It is not a path of dominance, but of discipline. It is not a path of glory, but of sacrifice. And most importantly, it is a path of balance. Only through balance will the world have a chance to thrive again."

The heavens grew still as Brahma's gaze turned to each of the Seven Sages. His eyes, brimming with infinite wisdom, seemed to see not just their outward forms but their innermost selves. Each sage felt the cosmic weight of his stare, as if Brahma were peering directly into the core of their being, examining the very essence of their worth and purpose.

Rudrayan – The Hammer of Justice

"Rudrayan," Brahma began, his voice reverberating through the heavens like the tolling of a distant bell. His eyes, filled with the ancient wisdom of creation, turned toward the tallest of the Seven Sages. A divine presence, Rudrayan stood, his broad shoulders brimming with strength, his deep-set eyes reflecting the weight of a thousand battles fought in the name of righteousness. In his hand, he held a massive mace—a symbol of his unyielding commitment to justice. But Brahma knew, as all the gods did, that even the mightiest weapons must be wielded with caution.

"You are the embodiment of justice," Brahma continued, his gaze unrelenting. "Your mace carries the weight of righteousness, but without wisdom, it can become an instrument of destruction. Your task is to restore justice to the world, but you must not act in blind fury. Seek not retribution, but restoration. Justice is not just in punishment, but in understanding the reasons behind each transgression."

The sky seemed to grow still, as if holding its breath, waiting for Rudrayan's response. The weight of Brahma's words sank into his chest, and for the first time, the true scope of his role began to settle upon him. His eyes glinted with the resolve of a warrior who had fought countless battles, but now, the battlefield was different. It was not one of blood and vengeance, but of understanding and healing.

Rudrayan's heart stirred with a mixture of pride and apprehension. His grip tightened around the handle of his mace, as though it were both a comfort and a burden. He had always believed that justice was the force that could right all wrongs, that it could vanquish evil with the power of righteousness. But now, he was being asked to see beyond the act of retribution, to peer into the hearts of those who had transgressed.

"I will carry this burden," Rudrayan declared, his voice steady but tinged with quiet uncertainty. *"But how can I know when my judgment is just, and when it is driven by my own rage?"*

Brahma's gaze softened, as if he understood the storm that brewed within Rudrayan's heart. He looked into the sage's eyes, as though seeing the very essence of his spirit laid bare. *"You must learn to temper your anger with understanding,"* Brahma said, his voice gentle but firm. *"For the world is broken, and only when you see the shattered pieces of others will you be able to piece them together again."*

The words struck Rudrayan like a bolt of lightning. He had always been quick to act, to punish, to strike down those who had wronged the world. But now, the very idea of justice itself seemed more complex, more nuanced. *"But how will I know when to act?"* Rudrayan asked, the weight of the uncertainty clear in his voice. *"How can I tell when my fury is justified, and when it will only deepen the wounds of the world?"*

Brahma nodded slowly, his eyes filled with ancient sorrow. *"That is your true challenge, Rudrayan. Your mace, while powerful, is not your greatest weapon. It is your heart. You must learn to listen—not just to the words of the guilty, but to the silence in their eyes, to the reasons behind their actions. Look not at the surface, but at the wounds that lie beneath. Injustice does not always come from malice. Sometimes, it is born of desperation, of fear, of pain."*

Rudrayan's brow furrowed in deep contemplation. The words seemed to twist and turn in his mind, the weight of responsibility growing heavier with each passing moment. To be a hammer of justice was one thing—to be the hand that shaped it with mercy was another.

"What if I am deceived?" Rudrayan asked, his voice laced with concern. *"What if my heart leads me astray, or if my judgment is clouded by the very fury you wish me to temper?"*

Brahma's eyes shone with the wisdom of the ages. *"That is why your task will not be a solitary one,"* he said. *"You must seek counsel, not just from other sages, but from the world itself. In every act of justice, there must be an act of self-reflection. Look within yourself, Rudrayan. Are you acting out of vengeance, or are you seeking to restore the balance that has been lost?"*

The weight of those words hung in the air, and for a long moment, Rudrayan said nothing. He understood now that his path was not one of simply wielding power—it was one of patience, introspection, and deep empathy. It was not about the punishment he could mete out, but about the healing that could be achieved by understanding the roots of the injustice.

"But how will I know when to forgive?" Rudrayan asked softly, the words foreign to him. Forgiveness had never been a part of his nature—justice, yes, but mercy had always felt like a compromise.

Brahma smiled, a small, knowing smile. *'Forgiveness is not weakness, Rudrayan. It is the strength to release the past and allow healing to take place. Forgiveness does not negate justice—it completes it. It is the final step in the process of restoration, the bridge that leads to true peace."*

Rudrayan's heart stirred again, this time with a growing sense of understanding. The path of justice was not one that could be walked with blind fury—it required wisdom, patience, and above all, compassion. The hammer he wielded would not merely strike down wrongdoers; it would shape the world into something greater, something more balanced, something that could heal.

He took a deep breath, feeling the weight of his mace in his hand, and nodded solemnly. *"I understand, Brahma,"* he said, his voice filled with newfound resolve. *"I will seek balance. I will learn to see the world through the eyes of those who suffer, and through my judgment, I will bring restoration, not destruction."*

Brahma's gaze softened further, his approval evident. *"That is the path of true justice, Rudrayan. Go now, and restore the world. But remember, justice is a delicate balance—it can save or it can destroy. You must be ever watchful, ever mindful of your heart, for it is both your guide and your greatest challenge."*

With that, Rudrayan bowed his head in reverence, feeling the weight of his task settle upon him like the very heavens themselves. He had been chosen to restore justice, but this was no simple task. It was a path of wisdom, compassion, and understanding—a path that would test his very soul. And with his mace in hand and a heart tempered by Brahma's guidance, he stepped forward, ready to face the trials that lay ahead.

Satyavrat – The Bearer of Truth

Brahma's attention shifted to Satyavrat, who stood with unwavering resolve, his silver eyes piercing through the very fabric of existence as though he could see the truth hidden beneath all things. His tall figure exuded a quiet strength, and his staff, a simple yet powerful symbol of his calling, rested firmly in his hand. The weight of his purpose settled upon him like an ancient mantle—one that would demand more than just the clarity of mind, but the clarity of heart.

"Satyavrat," Brahma's voice boomed through the ether, rich and deep, *"you are the Keeper of Truth. But truth, as you*

know, is often unwelcome, and it is not always easy to carry. There is a great burden in your role. You will not be received with open arms by all. Some will run from you, others will deny you, and there will be times when the truth you reveal will be seen as a threat rather than a gift."

Satyavrat's chest rose and fell with the steady rhythm of his breath, his heart unwavering even as the weight of Brahma's words pressed down on him. He had always known the price of truth, the loneliness it sometimes demanded, and the pain it often inflicted upon others. Yet, he also knew that truth was the foundation upon which all healing rested. It was the first step, the spark that could ignite the fires of transformation.

"I understand," Satyavrat replied, his voice steady, but tinged with the resolve that had guided him through countless trials. "I have seen the consequences of truth being rejected. I have witnessed the agony of those who could not bear to face it. Yet, I still believe in its power to heal. I still believe that in revealing the truth, even if it breaks the heart, we make room for the possibility of redemption."

Brahma's gaze softened as he studied the sage. The ancient deity knew that Satyavrat was no stranger to pain, but there was a quiet nobility in the way he carried it. He could see the unwavering conviction in the sage's heart, but Brahma also knew that the path ahead would be far from simple.

"Then you must carry that belief," Brahma said, his tone gentle but firm, *"even when the world resists. You will be tested in ways you cannot yet foresee. There will be moments when you*

question whether the truth you reveal is worth the pain it causes. In those moments, when your heart is torn by the suffering of others, remember this—truth is the first step toward healing. Without it, there can be no true justice, no true redemption."

The heavens seemed to hold their breath as Brahma's words echoed through the vastness of the universe. A deep silence followed, as if the cosmos itself were waiting for Satyavrat's response.

Satyavrat's grip tightened around his staff, and he stood taller, as though Brahma's words had ignited a flame within him. *"I understand the weight of this task, Lord,"* he said, his voice a low, steady murmur. *"But I will not turn from it. I will bring the truth, even if it shatters the very foundations of the world. It is only through facing the truth that we can find a path to redemption. The world may resist, but I will not falter. I will carry the burden, because it is a burden that must be borne."*

Brahma nodded, his expression one of quiet approval. *"It is not an easy task you have been given, Satyavrat. But you have the heart to endure it. There will be those who will see you as an enemy, those who will label you as a destroyer, as a bringer of chaos. But remember, you are the bearer of a great light. And the darkness of ignorance can only be dispelled by the harshest light of all—truth."*

Satyavrat lowered his head, a silent promise forming in his heart. *"I will be the light,"* he murmured. *"I will be the torchbearer, no matter how dark the path may seem. I will walk it, and I will guide others to walk it as well."*

Brahma's gaze softened further, his ancient eyes filled with a deep, unspoken understanding. *"You must understand,*

Satyavrat, that there will be times when the world will not be ready for the truth you carry. People will cling to their lies because they are more comfortable than the uncomfortable reality you will reveal. But in the face of such resistance, you must stand firm. The truth will eventually carve its own path, and you must be its unwavering guide."

Satyavrat raised his head, his silver eyes gleaming with quiet resolve. *"I will not turn back, Lord. I will not allow the world to remain shackled in the chains of falsehood."*

Brahma gave a final nod of approval before turning his attention to the other sages. *"Your path will not be an easy one, but it is necessary. The world is broken, and only truth can piece it back together. Go now, Satyavrat, and fulfill your role. Let truth be your shield and your sword. Let it be the foundation upon which the new world is built."*

As Brahma spoke these final words, a radiant light surrounded Satyavrat, enveloping him in a golden aura that seemed to emanate from the very core of the universe. He felt the weight of his task settle upon him like a mantle, and yet, within that weight, there was a strength—an unshakable resolve to fulfill his role as the Keeper of Truth.

The moment was fleeting, yet timeless, as the echoes of Brahma's words settled into Satyavrat's heart, etching themselves there with the clarity of the deepest conviction. He turned his gaze toward the ruined earth below, his heart steadfast, knowing that he would face unimaginable trials. But within the quiet depth of his soul, he carried the unwavering belief that the truth, though painful, would one day set the world free.

As the celestial assembly watched, Brahma's final command resounded like a clarion call: *"Go now, Satyavrat. Your task has begun."*

With one final glance at the cosmic trinity, Satyavrat stepped forward, his heart burning with the resolve to carry the truth to a world in need of healing.

Anirvan – The Silent Flame

Anirvan, The Flame of Courage, stood tall, his presence a living inferno of raw strength and indomitable will. His body crackled with energy, and his fingers, poised in the air, seemed to weave trails of fire as though his very essence burned with purpose. His chest heaved with steady breaths, and his eyes, sharp and unwavering, stared ahead as though the world itself would bend to the force of his courage. But within him, doubt began to stir—a whisper, small but persistent, questioning whether he was truly ready to bear the immense responsibility placed upon him.

Brahma's eyes—deep and infinite—shifted from the rest of the sages to Anirvan, his gaze a mixture of compassion and challenge. The Creator's voice resonated in the ether, each word vibrating through the very fabric of existence, filling the space with gravitas.

"Anirvan," Brahma began, his voice steady and commanding, yet laced with the subtle authority of one who had witnessed the rise and fall of countless ages, *"you are the flame of courage. The fire that will reignite hope in hearts that have been darkened by despair. It is your task to inspire those who have lost their will to fight, to dream, and to believe in themselves again."*

Anirvan stood a little straighter, feeling the weight of Brahma's words settle into him like the warmth of a furnace. He was no stranger to courage—he had led warriors into battle, fought battles that seemed unwinnable, and stared down the deepest fears with unflinching resolve. His heart surged with pride at the task before him. But Brahma's next words immediately cast a shadow upon that pride, reminding him of the depth and complexity of his mission.

"But listen carefully," Brahma continued, his voice darkening with caution, *"courage alone is not enough to save the world. It must be tempered with wisdom. Recklessness, the kind that is born from unchecked ego and blind will, is not bravery—it is destruction in the making. A fire, if left untended, can destroy everything in its path, even the things it was meant to protect."*

Anirvan's expression faltered for a fraction of a second. His heart, once so sure of itself, now raced with the weight of this new understanding. He had always believed that the strength of his courage, his unwavering resolve, would be enough to rally the lost souls of the world. But Brahma's words rang true—he had seen, in countless lives, the devastation wrought by misplaced bravery, by those who charged blindly into the fray, thinking only of the glory of battle without regard for the cost.

"I understand," Anirvan said, his voice steady but filled with an undercurrent of uncertainty. *"I will never falter in my duty to ignite courage in others. But how do I know when my fire burns too brightly, when it consumes rather than inspires? How do I distinguish between the flame of bravery and the inferno of folly?"*

Brahma studied him, the silence between them growing long and weighty. Then, with a deep, ancient sigh, Brahma spoke again, his voice softer now, yet filled with the weight of countless eons of wisdom.

"You must learn to listen to the subtle signs within your heart," Brahma said, his voice reverberating with timeless knowledge. *"True courage is not a loud, roaring flame; it is the quiet, steady warmth that gives light to those who have lost their way. A warrior who rushes into battle without thought, without consideration for the lives he will affect, does not fight for justice. He fights for glory, for his own pride. And that pride will blind him to the suffering his actions may cause. It is your responsibility to guide the hearts of others, to show them that courage does not mean fighting without cause, but standing firm in the face of adversity, knowing when to advance and when to hold back."*

Anirvan's heart beat a little faster as Brahma's words penetrated the depths of his mind. It was not enough to burn brightly; he must also learn to temper that fire, to wield it with the kind of foresight that could save lives, rather than sacrifice them recklessly.

"You will be called upon to inspire others—men, women, children— who are broken by the weight of their circumstances. You will show them the path forward, even when the road seems dark and fraught with danger. But remember, Anirvan, that courage is not just about taking action. It is about knowing when action is required, and when patience, understanding, and compassion are the true flames that must light the way."

Anirvan closed his eyes for a moment, allowing Brahma's wisdom to settle deeply within him. The flames that had always burned within him now flickered in a new light, one that he had never fully understood until this moment. He could feel the burning desire to charge forward, to lead the charge into battle, to inspire others through sheer strength and power. But Brahma had shown him the greater task—that true courage was not simply the act of battling external enemies, but the ability to conquer one's own impulses, to hold back the fire when necessary, and to trust that there was wisdom in restraint.

Anirvan opened his eyes, meeting Brahma's gaze with a newfound clarity.

"I will learn to balance my fire," Anirvan said with a newfound conviction, his voice steady and determined. *"I will guide those I encounter, not with reckless abandon, but with a heart that knows when to act and when to wait. I will learn the difference between the fire that burns for justice and the one that destroys without cause."*

Brahma nodded slowly, a hint of approval flickering in his eyes. *"Your path will not be easy, Anirvan. There will be times when you will be tempted to charge ahead, to fight without thought, to burn with passion until all is consumed. But in those moments, you must remember that courage, true courage, is the ability to stand firm when the world around you urges you to fall. It is the strength to act, but also the wisdom to know when not to act."*

Anirvan bowed his head in solemn respect, understanding that his role was not one of blind power, but of thoughtful, deliberate strength.

"I will do as you say, Brahma. I will carry this flame with wisdom, and I will ignite the hearts of others with a courage tempered by balance."

With those words, Brahma's gaze softened, as though he had placed a great weight upon Anirvan's shoulders—but one that was worthy of bearing. The Flame of Courage had been tasked with more than simply inspiring others; he had been entrusted with the responsibility of learning restraint, of understanding that courage was not an unbridled force, but a disciplined energy that could shape the world.

As Anirvan turned to take his leave, his flame now flickering with a deeper understanding, Brahma's voice echoed in the silence that followed. *"Remember, Anirvan— only through balance will the true power of your flame be realized. Your courage will be your greatest gift and your greatest challenge. Walk the path wisely."*

Vidyatman – The Keeper of Knowledge

Vidyatman stood before Brahma, his form draped in robes that shimmered with the ethereal light of countless ages. The fabric seemed to reflect the wisdom of a thousand lifetimes, each thread woven with the stories of civilizations long forgotten. His eyes, ancient and knowing, held the depth of all the knowledge he had gathered over eons. Yet, despite his vast intellect, he was burdened by the weight of the very gift that defined him—the knowledge that he had acquired but never truly shared. The mantle of his title, *"The Keeper of Knowledge," felt heavy on his shoulders, as though the vast library of the universe was compressed into his very soul.*

Brahma's gaze fixed on him, and the creator's voice resonated in the infinite space between them. *"Vidyatman, knowledge is a powerful force. But knowledge without compassion can become a prison. Your task is to bring understanding to the world, to help others see the truths they cannot yet comprehend. But beware—wisdom can bind as much as it can free."*

The words hung in the air, each syllable a cosmic truth. Vidyatman felt a shudder ripple through his being, as if the universe itself had trembled at the weight of the Creator's command. His lips parted slightly, as though to speak, but he remained silent, overwhelmed by the realization that his life's purpose had just shifted from the pursuit of knowledge to its purposeful dissemination.

"How am I to teach the world?" Vidyatman's voice, though calm, trembled slightly, a rare vulnerability breaking through his usually

serene exterior. "I have sought knowledge through countless paths, yet never before have I been asked to guide others to its light. How can one make others see, when they are blind to the very truth I carry?"

Brahma's eyes softened, his four faces reflecting different aspects of the cosmos as they gazed upon Vidyatman. The Creator's voice was gentle, but the weight of his words hung heavily in the air. *"That is your challenge, Vidyatman. You must teach others to see the world clearly—not as you see it, for each person has their own vision—but through their own experiences. You must help them understand not only the facts, but the deeper truths that lie beneath them. Only then will knowledge have its full power. And remember, wisdom that is forced upon others only imprisons them further. It must be given with compassion, not as a weapon, but as a tool for liberation."*

Vidyatman's mind swirled with questions and doubts, the paradox of his mission pressing upon him. He had spent countless lifetimes in isolation, studying, absorbing, and categorizing the vast storehouses of wisdom. Yet in his pursuit of understanding, he had never truly questioned whether the knowledge he had obtained was meant to be shared or whether it was a burden to those who were unprepared to bear it.

He closed his eyes in quiet contemplation, the silence of the universe surrounding him. For a long moment, he stood there, enveloped in the enormity of Brahma's task. Then, he spoke again, his voice steady but full of introspection. *"I have spent countless lifetimes seeking knowledge, but I fear that in my search, I may have imprisoned myself in the very wisdom I sought to share. I have become so consumed by the pursuit of truth that I have forgotten the compassion that must accompany it. If my wisdom remains unattainable or misunderstood, how can I possibly help others?"*

Brahma's gaze grew more intense, the divine wisdom within him apparent as he looked into Vidyatman's soul. *"That is the burden you must bear, Vidyatman. The knowledge you carry is vast, but it must be shared with humility and patience. Your gift is not in merely presenting facts but in understanding when to speak and when to listen. Your true power will be in your ability to guide others on their own paths of discovery, not to impose your wisdom upon them."*

Vidyatman's heart fluttered as Brahma's words began to pierce through the veil of his doubts. He understood, then, that his role was not to be a dispenser of answers, but a guide—a lantern to illuminate the path for others to walk, each step taken at their own pace. His wisdom was not a prison to be locked away, nor was it a treasure to be hoarded. It was a key to unlock the door of understanding for others.

"But what if they do not understand?" Vidyatman asked, his voice strained. *"What if they resist the knowledge I offer, unable to see the truth I wish to impart?"*

Brahma's expression remained calm, his voice resonating with the timeless wisdom of the cosmos. *"That is the nature of knowledge, Vidyatman. It is not always welcomed with open arms, for it challenges the very foundations of what one believes to be true. Some will reject it. Others will cling to their ignorance, for it is comfortable to remain in the dark. But your duty is not to force them into the light—it is to show them that the light exists. It is to make them curious, to awaken within them the desire to seek their own truths."*

Vidyatman's heart began to ease, the heavy burden of his doubt beginning to shift into something lighter—a sense of purpose, of clarity. He understood now that his task was not to impose his wisdom but to create space for others to learn and grow, to help them see the world with eyes unclouded by prejudice or fear. His knowledge could serve as a mirror, reflecting the truths that were already within others, helping them recognize their own potential.

"I understand, Brahma," Vidyatman said, his voice firm with newfound resolve. *"I must not simply give knowledge, but help others discover it within themselves. I will not be the keeper of wisdom alone, but the keeper of the process by which others come to understand. I will guide them, but I will not impose. I will offer the seed of knowledge, but allow them to plant it in their own hearts."*

Brahma nodded, the cosmic trinity above them glowing brighter as the heavens trembled in response. *"That is your path, Vidyatman. You will be the Keeper of Knowledge, but not as a solitary scholar. You will be a teacher, a mentor, a catalyst for awakening. But remember—if you hold your wisdom too tightly, it will lose its power. Wisdom must flow freely, like a river that nourishes all who drink from it. Guide them with patience, with compassion, and with the understanding that each soul must find their own way."*

As Brahma's words settled into his heart, Vidyatman took a deep breath, his soul brimming with purpose. The task before him was immense, but now he understood it fully. He was not merely a vessel of knowledge—he was a beacon, guiding others through the darkness, helping them find their own light. And with that understanding, the weight of his role seemed a little lighter. The Keeper of Knowledge would no longer be a solitary figure locked in a tower of wisdom, but a living testament to the power of understanding, shared freely and with compassion.

Karunesh – The Vessel of Mercy

Brahma's eyes turned to Karunesh, and the heavens seemed to quiet, as though all the celestial bodies awaited the words of the Creator. Karunesh stood before him, his presence marked by a serene yet sorrowful aura. His attire was a deep, oceanic blue, reflecting not only the vastness of the sky but the depths of his compassion. There was an aura of both wisdom and vulnerability around him, as if his very being carried the weight of every suffering soul he had ever encountered.

"Karunesh," Brahma began, his voice resonating through the cosmos with the clarity of truth, *"you are the Vessel of Mercy. Your heart overflows with compassion for all suffering, for all who are lost, for all who cry out in the darkness. You embody the very essence of mercy—the balm for wounds that are too deep to heal with simple gestures. You are called to comfort, to mend, to soothe, and to give hope."*

The words of Brahma hung in the air, heavy with the truth of Karunesh's task. The sage's heart swelled with the eternal burden of mercy, the kind that transcended mere pity or kindness. It was a profound gift, but one that also carried great responsibility.

"You are a healer of wounds, Karunesh. But," Brahma's voice deepened, *"mercy alone is not enough. Mercy without wisdom leads to weakness, to an inability to make the difficult choices that may bring true healing. To be merciful is noble, but mercy can become a curse if it is wielded without justice."*

A cold gust of wind passed through the space, carrying with it the remnants of the world's past, and Karunesh's eyes darkened with an ancient sorrow. He bowed his head, feeling the weight of Brahma's words. The truth pierced his heart, yet he knew that it was the truth he needed to hear.

"I understand," Karunesh said, his voice quiet, but filled with the strength that only years of suffering could forge. *"I have always believed that mercy is the antidote to pain. But... the world I now face is filled with complexities. How do I heal without enabling weakness? How do I bring comfort without making others dependent on my mercy?"*

Brahma's expression softened, his gaze filled with understanding. He spoke gently but firmly, *"You must learn, Karunesh, that true mercy is not the absence of strength. It is not the simple act of sheltering the wounded from the consequences of their actions. No, true mercy is the strength to know when to act, when to heal, and when to let go. It is the wisdom to recognize when mercy prolongs suffering, and when justice must take precedence."*

Karunesh's heart trembled at the thought. The idea that his mercy could prolong suffering seemed antithetical to everything he had ever believed. His entire being was dedicated to alleviating pain, to offering solace to those in need. To turn away, to withhold mercy at times, was a concept that shook him to his core.

"You speak of justice," Karunesh whispered, his voice barely audible, *"but how can I, who am defined by mercy, ever choose justice over compassion? How can I watch someone suffer when I know I can ease their pain?"*

Brahma's gaze never wavered. *"That, Karunesh, is the challenge. You will be tested, as all the sages will be. You will face situations where your compassion will cry out for release, where your heart will beg you to intervene. But mercy that is not tempered with justice can become an enabler of harm. Your role is not to protect those who refuse to face the consequences of their actions. You must decide when to extend a hand to heal, and when to let the world's natural order take its course."*

The words struck Karunesh like a blow. He felt the weight of every soul he had helped, every tear he had wiped away, and every wound he had tended to. But within that weight, a spark of clarity flickered—a truth that Brahma had planted within him.

"And what if I fail?" Karunesh asked, his voice thick with emotion. *"What if my mercy leads to harm, or worse, to suffering*

that could have been avoided? Can I bear that weight? Can I truly learn to balance mercy with justice?"

Brahma's voice softened, like the touch of a comforting breeze. *"Your heart will bleed, Karunesh. There is no denying that. But that is the price of mercy. The task before you is not to find the easy way out, nor to simply provide a temporary balm for pain. Your compassion will be tested time and again, and you will face moments where no answer is clear. But you must trust in your ability to discern, to act with wisdom, and to always hold justice in the same breath as mercy."*

He paused, allowing the gravity of his words to settle in. *"Remember, true mercy is not about endless forgiveness without consequence. It is about recognizing the potential for growth in others, even if that growth is painful. You will have to face the hardest choices, Karunesh. You will have to let go of those you wish to heal, for their own sake. Only then will you fulfill your task in Karma Yug—to create a balance where mercy guides without weakening the world, where justice and compassion walk side by side."*

The words hung in the air, and for a moment, Karunesh stood motionless, his eyes clouded with the weight of his task. The eternal conflict between mercy and justice was now his to carry. He felt as though his heart had been split in two—one side filled with the longing to comfort and soothe every wounded soul, the other now imbued with the wisdom to understand when to step back and allow others to face the consequences of their actions.

Karunesh finally lifted his head, his eyes now steely with determination, though the sorrow in them remained.

"I will bear this burden, Brahma," he said, his voice steady, yet filled with a deep melancholy. "Though it will break my heart many times, I will strive to learn this balance. I fear I will falter, for my heart bleeds for all who suffer. But I will not let that bleed become the end of their journey."

Brahma nodded, his four faces reflecting the wisdom of the universe. *"You will falter, Karunesh. But you will rise again. And in rising, you will teach the world that mercy is not an act of weakness, but an act of the greatest strength."*

The silence between them was thick with the weight of the task that now lay before Karunesh. As he stood, facing the uncertain path ahead, he felt the trembling of the earth beneath him. The world was broken, but it could be healed—through strength, through wisdom, and through a mercy that did not seek to protect from the consequences of one's actions, but to guide the soul to redemption.

Yuktashakti – The Weaver of Fate

Yuktashakti stood apart from the rest of the sages, her eyes sharp, gleaming with an intensity that seemed to see through the very fabric of reality. Around her, threads of shimmering light wove and tangled—an intricate web of destinies, infinite possibilities stretching out before her, each one seemingly within her reach. The threads danced in the air like an unspoken melody, swirling in a cosmic dance that only she could perceive. To others, the world might seem still, but to Yuktashakti, it was a living tapestry in constant flux, constantly shifting with every decision, every action, every breath taken.

Her fingers twitched as she instinctively reached out to touch the strands that hung in the air, but something held her back. She understood these threads—knew them as well as she knew her own heart. She could see the paths of the future, unfolding before her eyes in vivid clarity. Yet, in her mind, there lingered a question that had plagued her ever since she had received this gift: How much power could one have over fate before it was lost forever?

Brahma's voice echoed through the heavens, its profound resonance reverberating in the very air around them. *"Yuktashakti,"* he called, his words soft yet powerful, carrying with them the weight of the universe.

Yuktashakti straightened, her gaze still fixed on the weaving threads of destiny. She did not need to turn to face him to know that the Creator himself had addressed her. Her heart fluttered with a mixture of anticipation and anxiety. She had known this moment was coming, but now that it was here, the enormity of her role began to settle heavily upon her shoulders.

"You are the Weaver of Fate, Yuktashakti," Brahma continued, his voice like a divine current, steady and unyielding. *"The one who can see the strands of destiny, the invisible threads that bind all of existence together. But be warned—knowing the future*

is both a gift and a curse. You will have the power to influence the course of the world, to nudge it toward its rightful path, but you must be cautious. For fate is not yours to control. It is yours to influence, and that is where the balance lies."

Yuktashakti's heart skipped a beat. Her mind raced with the implications of Brahma's words. Not control, but influence. Her hands hovered near the threads, but she withdrew them quickly, as if they might burn her with their potential.

"I can see the future," she murmured, almost to herself, her voice carrying a trace of doubt. "But what if I am not meant to change it? What if my vision of fate is flawed? What if I am wrong?"

Brahma's voice softened, carrying a deep, understanding tone. *"That is your challenge, Yuktashakti. You must use your sight wisely, knowing when to intervene and when to let the world unfold on its own. You must be the guiding hand, but never the iron fist. The role of the Weaver is not one of domination, but of subtlety. You must guide, nudge, and redirect, but never force. Fate is not to be bound by a single will—it is meant to evolve. It is a living force, shaped by all who participate in it."*

Yuktashakti closed her eyes for a moment, her mind swirling with the weight of her responsibility. She had seen countless possibilities unfold before her—the rise of civilizations, the fall of empires, the birth of new worlds, the end of old ones. She had witnessed heroes and villains alike, their fates twisted and tangled within her threads, their lives shaped by forces beyond their control. Yet, now that it was her turn to wield the power of fate, she realized the delicate balance she had to maintain.

"You will shape the course of history, Yuktashakti," Brahma continued, his tone unwavering. *"But you must not allow your own desires, your own vision, to cloud your judgment. When you step into the weave, you must do so with humility, understanding that the threads you manipulate are not merely your own. They belong to every soul, every action, every choice that has ever been made or will ever be made."*

Yuktashakti's fingers twitched again, a momentary impulse to touch the threads, but she held back. *"How do I know when to intervene, and when to stand back?"* Her voice wavered with uncertainty, but there was a spark of determination in her eyes.

Brahma regarded her with a gaze that seemed to pierce into her very soul. *"You will know, Yuktashakti. It is not through calculation, but through understanding. You must trust the wisdom within you. When the threads tremble in a way that suggests a turning point—when a single action or choice could alter the course of an entire world—you must decide if the world is ready for that change. If it is, guide it. If not, allow the threads to untangle on their own. Never forget that fate is an ever-changing dance. Too much intervention will break it, too little will lead to stagnation."*

A deep silence fell between them as Yuktashakti absorbed Brahma's words, the weight of his wisdom settling like an anchor in her heart. The enormity of her task began to sink in. She was not to be a puppet master of the cosmos, pulling strings and directing the flow of existence according to her whims. No, she was to be the careful guide, the subtle hand that would help the world find its way, but never impose her will upon it.

"And one more thing," Brahma added, his voice a whisper now, as if he was imparting the final, most sacred piece of wisdom. *"Beware, Yuktashakti, for those who see too much of the future often find themselves trapped by it. The threads of fate can be a prison as much as they are a path. Do not allow yourself to become so consumed by the future that you forget to live in the present. The world needs you to be both its guide and its witness."*

Yuktashakti stood motionless for a long moment, the weight of her duty pressing down on her with an intensity she had not anticipated. She could feel the threads of fate pulsing around her, their energy vibrating through her very being. There was a sense of foreboding in the air, but also an undeniable sense of purpose. Her task was clear now. She was to guide, not control; to influence, not dominate. She was the Weaver, and it was her duty to ensure the world moved in the right direction, but only by working within the delicate balance of fate itself.

With a deep breath, Yuktashakti opened her eyes, her gaze now steady and unwavering. She was ready. She knew that the path ahead would not be easy, but she also knew that this was her destiny. And she would weave it, thread by thread, with all the wisdom she could gather.

"I understand," she said, her voice firm, a quiet determination in her tone. *"I will guide the world, Brahma. I will shape its fate, but I will not force it. I will be its weaver, not its master."*

Brahma's four faces smiled softly, the corners of his lips curling in a rare expression of approval. *"Go then, Yuktashakti, the Weaver of Fate. Guide the world with your wisdom, and may the threads of destiny unfold as they were always meant to."*

With that, Yuktashakti stepped forward, her hands extended to touch the threads of destiny, ready to fulfill her purpose. She would not control the future—she would guide it, and in doing so, ensure that the world would find its true path in the vast, ever-changing weave of fate.

Nirvansh – The Master of Desire

The heavens fell silent as Brahma's gaze shifted to Nirvansh, the Sage of Mastery Over Desire. His deep, wise eyes, pools of infinite knowledge, bore into Nirvansh's soul, as if reading the very essence of his being. Nirvansh, standing tall yet inwardly conflicted, felt the weight of the Creator's words before they were even spoken. The air hummed with the gravity of his role.

"Nirvansh," Brahma's voice echoed, rich and steady, vibrating through the cosmos like a steady heartbeat. *"Desire is the force that drives all things. It fuels creation and, if left unchecked, can lead to destruction. Your task is to help the world understand desire—not to suppress it, nor to indulge it, but to master it. Desire without control leads to suffering, but desire without purpose leads to stagnation. You must teach the world that balance is the key."*

As Brahma's words reverberated in the air, Nirvansh's mind flickered with memories of his past life, his time as Vasujit—the human who had once grappled with desire in its most unrestrained form. His heart sank as he recalled the emptiness that followed after every indulgence, every moment of craving that had left him more hollow than before.

He glanced down at the cracked earth beneath him, his thoughts drifting to the long years spent in turmoil and confusion. Desire had once consumed him completely, a flame that burned without purpose, without end. How could he teach others about balance when he himself had struggled so deeply with desire?

Nirvansh's voice was soft, almost a whisper, laden with the weight of his internal battle. *"I have seen the depths of longing, Brahma—the emptiness that follows desire. I have known the insatiable hunger that gnaws at the soul, the yearning that nothing can satisfy. How can I show others the way when I, too, struggle with my own desires?"*

Brahma's eyes softened, reflecting the vast compassion that only the Creator could possess. His voice, though still firm, was filled with understanding. *"You have learned the hardest lesson, Nirvansh. To understand desire is to understand the heart of the universe. It is through your own struggles that you have gained the wisdom necessary to guide others. You must teach the world to balance their desires with their actions. Help them see the difference between want and need, between fleeting cravings and lasting fulfillment. That is your task, and it will be the greatest challenge of all."*

Nirvansh felt a surge of conflicting emotions. He had been chosen not in spite of his struggles with desire but because of them. It was in the crucible of his own inner conflict that he had learned the deepest truths. But how would he impart this to a world so desperate for instant gratification? How could he teach mastery over something so all-consuming?

His voice, now steady with resolve, rose to meet Brahma's. *"I understand the burden of desire as few others can. I will do my best, but the task is daunting. The world does not seek mastery—it seeks indulgence. Desire runs through every fiber of their being like an unquenchable fire. To master it requires more than understanding; it requires transformation."*

Brahma nodded, his expression serene yet resolute. *"Indeed, Nirvansh. The path ahead will be fraught with resistance, but it is your duty to help the world see that mastery over desire is not about renunciation, but about empowerment. Only when desire is understood can it be transformed into something that serves the greater good. Your task is to show them that desire, in its purest form, can be a force for creation, for growth, for evolution."*

Nirvansh, though still troubled by the enormity of the challenge, felt a flicker of hope in his heart. He had spent lifetimes consumed by desire, unable to break free from its chains. But now, as the Master of Desire, he had the power to not only master his own cravings but to show others the way to freedom as well.

Brahma continued, his voice now taking on a tone of deeper wisdom. *"To master desire, Nirvansh, you must first teach the world the art of discernment. Help them understand the difference between true fulfillment and the hollow pursuit of excess. Show them that desire, when aligned with purpose, can lead to true satisfaction, but when left unchecked, it can only lead to ruin."*

A pause lingered in the air, the weight of the words settling like dust after a great storm. Nirvansh, his gaze steady and intense, nodded slowly, understanding the depth of the Creator's instruction. The task before him was monumental, but it was also transformative. To help the world find balance, to show them the way of desire's mastery, was to help them reclaim their own destinies.

Brahma's eyes narrowed, and for a brief moment, it was as though the universe itself held its breath. *"You must also remember, Nirvansh,"* Brahma added, *his voice taking on a sharper edge, "that mastering desire is not just about controlling the self, but about guiding others to control theirs. You will be tested, as you were tested in your past life. The very force of desire will come against you, in forms both familiar and new. But it is in the face of these temptations that your true strength will shine."*

Nirvansh's heart fluttered at the thought of these tests. His past had been one of constant battle with his inner longings—how would he fare when the very force he sought to master came to challenge him again? Yet, despite the fear that gripped him, he felt a renewed determination rise within him.

"I will teach them, Brahma," he said, his voice firm and unwavering now. *"I will help them understand the value of their desires, guide them to distinguish between need and want. And*

above all, I will show them that mastery is not about denial, but about choice. We choose what to desire, and through that choice, we shape our own lives and the world around us."

Brahma's gaze softened further, a glimmer of approval shining through. *"Remember, Nirvansh,"* he said, *"true mastery comes not from rejecting desire, but from understanding it. You are the Master of Desire, but you are also its servant. Through you, the world will learn not to suppress their desires, but to channel them into something greater. Through you, the world will learn balance."*

As the Creator's voice faded into the cosmic ether, Nirvansh stood in the silence that followed, the weight of his task settling deeper into his soul. He understood now—this was not just about desire, but about transformation. His journey had only just begun, and the world would be his greatest teacher.

With one last glance at the broken earth beneath him, Nirvansh raised his gaze to the heavens, his heart burning with purpose. The age of Karma Yug had begun, and with it, the path of desire would be walked—not with indulgence, nor with denial, but with mastery.

The Path Forward

As Brahma finished speaking, the Seven Sages stood in solemn silence, their hearts heavy with the weight of their monumental task. Each of them understood the gravity of their responsibility, knowing that their every action would determine the fate of the world. Yet, despite the uncertainty and the vastness of the task ahead, a quiet resolve began to burn in their eyes. They had been chosen for their unique qualities, but the path that awaited them was one of unimaginable trials and tribulations. Their destiny, once clear and abstract, now stood before them as an untrodden road, fraught with obstacles, doubt, and peril.

Brahma looked down upon them, his four faces reflecting the full spectrum of creation. His deep, resonant voice echoed across the heavens, as though it were the very fabric of existence itself, speaking into the souls of each sage.

"Remember this," Brahma's voice rang out with undeniable authority, *"you are the architects of Karma Yug, the builders of a new world, but your task is not to shape it through power alone. You will mold it through understanding, through the subtle art of balance. The world lies in ruins because the old ways were led by force, by the misguided certainty of the divine. Now, you are here to guide the world through a new principle—karma, the law of actions and consequences."*

He paused, his gaze moving across the Seven Sages. His eyes, ancient and filled with the wisdom of countless aeons, seemed to peer into the very hearts of the sages.

"You are not gods of dominion, but of guidance. This will not be easy, and there will be times when you doubt your path, but know this—your purpose is greater than any fear, greater than any sorrow that may come your way. For every choice you make, every step you take, you will be the breath of life for the universe. You will rebuild what was lost."

The sages stood in awe, the weight of Brahma's words sinking in. It was not power that would shape the world, but purpose. And with that purpose came a burden—one that would demand everything from them.

But before they could respond, a new voice filled the heavens—a voice calm, steady, and unwavering.

Vishnu, the Preserver, appeared before them, his form bathed in the infinite blue glow of the cosmic ocean. His expression, serene yet resolute, reflected an eternal patience, as though he had already seen the outcome of this moment in the timeless tapestry of the universe. His eyes, deep and wise, locked with the sages, and his voice, like a calm sea, washed over them.

"Brahma speaks truly," Vishnu said. "But know this, O Sages of Karma Yug, you will not walk this path alone. You will have my guidance, the quiet strength of the tides, which move through all things, whether visible or hidden. The world you will create will be balanced, not by the weight of dominance, but by the rhythm of preservation. You will guide the world not by shaping every destiny, but by letting each soul find its own path, as the tides shape the shore without ever forcing it."

Vishnu's words, so full of wisdom, soothed the anxiety of the sages, their hearts finding a moment of peace in the understanding that the weight of creation would not be borne by them alone. His voice softened, but there was no mistaking the authority in his words.

"You will be the preservers of Karma Yug," Vishnu continued. "You must understand that not all things will go as planned. There

will be turmoil, chaos, and struggle. But that is the nature of balance. For every action, there will be a counteraction. And as the ocean sustains all life, so too will you, through patience and wisdom, ensure that Karma Yug survives."

The Seven Sages, moved by Vishnu's presence, stood taller. Their resolve was firm, for Vishnu's words reminded them that even in the chaos, there was a guiding force—a deep, eternal rhythm that would carry them through.

Then, from the fiery depths of the cosmos, came a voice—fierce, unrelenting, and full of primal strength. Shiva, the Destroyer, appeared before them, his presence a tempest of divine fire, his eyes burning with the intensity of a thousand suns. He was not a god of destruction for its own sake, but for the creation that emerged from it, and his words were imbued with the raw power of transformation.

"You stand before me, Seven Sages," Shiva spoke, his voice like the rumble of thunder, "and you fear the task ahead. But let me tell you this—you must learn to embrace destruction. Not destruction in the sense of annihilation, but destruction as transformation. The world has already fallen. What you build must be forged in the fires of your will, tempered in the heat of your doubts. Do not be afraid to burn away what is unnecessary, to destroy what no longer serves the greater balance. From the ashes of the old will the new arise."

The fire around Shiva flickered and flared, illuminating the heavens with its intensity. The air vibrated with his words, charged with a deep, untamable energy.

"Your path is one of balance. You must understand that creation and destruction are not opposites, but two sides of the same coin. It is only through destruction that creation can emerge. Your task, then, is not to preserve what was, but to transform the broken remnants into something new—something worthy of Karma Yug."

Shiva's words resonated deeply with the Seven Sages. Each of them knew that their journey would require them to make difficult choices, and some would demand the destruction of old ways to make room for new growth. Shiva's blessing, fierce and wild, emboldened them.

Finally, Brahma spoke once more, his voice steady, unwavering. *"Together, you will guide the universe. You will not face the trials ahead alone. Vishnu, the Preserver, will give you patience, and I, Brahma, will offer you the wisdom to see the threads of destiny. Shiva, the Destroyer, will grant you the strength to tear down that which no longer serves the world. The gods who stand in the heavens will watch over you, but it is you—each of you—who must shape the world."*

He turned toward the other gods, his voice now taking on an authoritative tone, commanding yet filled with conviction.

"Other gods may doubt you, question the wisdom of Karma Yug. But I say to them—look upon these Seven Sages, for they carry the weight of the universe's future. They are the ones who will rebuild, not by divine power, but by the strength of their actions, their choices, and their will to restore balance. Trust in them. Have faith in their vision, for it is through their efforts that the universe will find its balance once again."

As Brahma spoke, Vishnu nodded in quiet agreement, his calm eyes gleaming with the knowledge that the time had come for the Seven Sages to walk their path. Shiva, too, gave a small, approving smile—an acknowledgment of the fierceness that would be required to rebuild what had been lost.

And with that, the Seven Sages—Rudrayan, Satyavrat, Anirvan, Vidyatman, Karunesh, Yuktashakti, and Nirvansh—felt the weight of the divine presence surrounding them. They were not alone. The gods had entrusted them with the rebirth of the universe, and they would carry the vision of Karma Yug forward with strength, wisdom, patience, and transformation.

The world was in ruins. But the dawn of Karma Yug had arrived, and with it, the hope of a new beginning. The Seven Sages turned towards their future, their destinies now intertwined with the fate of all existence. Their journey had begun.

And thus, the silence of the heavens birthed a new rhythm—one not sung by gods, but woven by mortals. Through justice, through truth, through courage and restraint, through mercy and wisdom, through fate and desire—they would script a world that remembers: it is not the divine that redeems creation, but the choices of the awakened soul.

Chapter 3

The Trials of the Chosen

A thick mist swirled around the seven sages as they stood in the sacred void between realms, their forms barely visible in the dim glow of cosmic energy. They had spoken their truths, revealed their doubts, yet the gods remained silent. Then, as if the universe itself had exhaled, three celestial figures emerged from the darkness—Brahma, Vishnu, and Shiva. Their eyes held the weight of creation, preservation, and destruction, and in their gazes lay a challenge unspoken yet understood.

Vishnu stepped forward, his voice neither harsh nor kind, but absolute. *"You have been chosen, yet you still question yourselves. If you are to forge Karma Yug, you must first conquer the ghosts of your own karma. But tell me, sages—do you doubt your worth, or do you doubt the very path you must walk? Are you bound by fear of failure, or do you still seek a higher truth?"* His gaze swept over them, piercing through their silence. *"What will you do when the weight of your choices is heavier than the heavens themselves? When justice and mercy clash, when duty and love stand opposed—will you waver, or will you stand firm? Answer me, for Karma Yug will not be built by those who falter in the face of their own doubts!"*

With a wave of his hand, the space around them shattered into fragments of time. Each shard twisted, forming individual realms—one for each sage. One by one, they were pulled into their pasts, each facing the trial that would determine if they were truly worthy.

Rudrayan: The Weight of Judgment

Rudrayan had grown up in the shadow of injustice, his childhood a battlefield of its own. Born into a dynasty that ruled with an iron fist, he had watched his father dispense judgment without mercy, crushing the weak beneath his rule. He had seen men hanged for stealing a loaf of bread, women stoned for defying the word of their masters, and children left orphaned by the whims of power.

From a young age, Rudrayan had wrestled with the meaning of justice. He had trained in combat not for conquest, but for the strength to protect. He had studied laws, scriptures, and philosophies, hoping to find a path where power did not corrupt. Yet, deep within him, the flames of vengeance simmered. He had once believed justice was a clear blade, striking down the wicked without hesitation. But as he grew, he realized—justice was not simple. It was heavy, tangled in duty and emotion.

And now, as the scent of burning flesh filled his nostrils, Rudrayan stood upon a field of corpses, his breath ragged, his heart pounding like war drums. The air was thick with the stench of death, blood seeping into the earth as if the land itself wept. His sword, slick with crimson, pulsed in his grip—an extension of his rage, his duty, his burden.

Before him, on his knees, was his father. Once a towering force of tyranny, now reduced to a pleading man, his proud gaze shattered into fear. The same hands that had crushed the weak now trembled, fingers clutching at the dirt as if the very earth could shield him from fate. The same voice that had commanded execution now whispered, cracked with desperation, *"Will you not grant mercy, my son?"*

Tears, unbidden and raw, welled in the old man's eyes. *"I raised you to be strong, to never waver. Have you grown so cold that you cannot see the man before you is not a king, not a ruler—just a father who has lost his way?" His voice broke, his body shaking. "I am no longer the tyrant you despised, Rudrayan. I am just a man. Your father. I beg you, let me live. Let me atone. Give me the mercy I never gave to others."*

The great warrior, the Flame of Justice, stood frozen. His breath was shallow, his pulse roaring in his ears. This was the man who had once ruled with an iron fist, who had laughed as families were torn apart, who had relished the fear in the eyes of those he sentenced to death. This was the man who had mocked his own son's ideals, calling mercy a fool's weakness, justice a plaything of the weak.

And yet now, kneeling in the dust, he was no more than a broken soul, his proud, arrogant face streaked with tears. *"Please, my son," he sobbed, his voice raw and trembling. "I was blind. I was cruel. But I am still your father. Do you not have even a shred of love left for me? Spare me! Let me atone! I beg you!"*

Rudrayan's grip tightened around his sword, his knuckles white. His father had never begged for anything—never bowed, never pleaded. He had ordered executions like a man ordering a meal, had scoffed at suffering as if it were a mere inconvenience. Now, he grovelled, clutching at his son's feet, his voice breaking like a man drowning in his own sins.

The words struck like a dagger. Rudrayan had long dreamt of this moment—of bringing justice, of ending the reign of terror that had consumed his people. And yet, staring into the eyes of the man who had shaped him, his fury clashed with something deeper. Love? Duty? The ghost of a child who had once longed for his father's approval?

His grip on the sword tightened, muscles rigid with conflict. *"Does justice leave space for mercy?"* he muttered, his voice raw, as if torn from his very soul.

A storm raged within him—anger intertwined with sorrow, vengeance tangled with love. Was he the executioner or the redeemer? The warrior or the son? Would denying him mercy make Rudrayan the just ruler he had always aspired to be—or merely another tyrant, no different from the man before him??

A deep voice echoed through the heavens—Shiva's voice, resonant and commanding. *"Karma is neither blind nor cruel, Rudrayan. But do you know if your justice is truly righteous? Or is it only vengeance with a noble name?"* His words carried both challenge and wisdom, like thunder rolling through the skies. In the silence that followed, the air thickened with an ancient gravity.

The stars themselves seemed to pause, bearing witness to the trial unfolding. The presence of the divine was no longer a distant echo—it pressed against Rudrayan's soul like thunder held in suspense, waiting for his truth to rise above rage.

Shiva stepped forward, his celestial form towering, his third eye flickering with restrained energy. *"Tell me, Rudrayan,"* he continued, his voice softer yet no less intense, *"Does justice exist without compassion? Would you wield the sword of righteousness if it stripped you of your own humanity?"*

Rudrayan's breath hitched, his grip tightening around the hilt of his weapon. *"I fight for the innocent, for those who suffered beneath his rule! How can I allow him to live, knowing the agony he has caused?"*

Shiva's gaze pierced through him. *"Then tell me, warrior, when you look into his eyes now, do you still see only a tyrant? Or do you see a broken man who, for the first time, understands the weight of his sins? Will you strike him down as an enemy—or rise above, as something greater?"*

The words struck Rudrayan deeper than any blade ever could. The battlefield was silent, save for the ragged breathing of a father pleading for his life and a son torn between justice and mercy.

The sword trembled in his grasp. The choice lay before him, heavier than the blade in his hands.

"Will you not grant mercy, my son?" the man whispered, voice trembling. *"Does justice leave no space for forgiveness?"*

The choice lay before him, heavier than the sword in his hand. His breath was shallow, his grip unsteady. The fire of vengeance burned within him, yet the embers of love still flickered in the depths of his soul. A storm raged in his heart, his father's broken pleas colliding with the screams of the countless lives he had ruined. The tyrant before him was now a mere shadow of the man who had ruled with arrogance and cruelty.

Satyavrat: The Tyranny of Truth

Satyavrat had been raised in a household where truth was not just valued, but worshipped. His father, Sage Rishabh, was known far and wide as a man who would rather endure suffering than utter a single falsehood. *"Truth is the foundation of existence,"* he would say, his voice echoing in the halls of their simple yet sacred dwelling. *"A man who compromises on truth has already lost himself."*

As a child, Satyavrat had watched his father refuse favors from kings, reject luxuries, and stand unwavering even when truth led to hardship. He had witnessed his father denounce a powerful ruler for deceiving his people, even when it meant exile. *"A truth untold is a lie in disguise,"* his father had taught him, his voice resolute, his eyes filled with conviction.

His mother, gentle yet firm, had always reminded him, *"Truth is the light, my son. But even light can blind if it is too harsh."* Yet, his father would counter, *"But without truth, there is only darkness. Better to be blinded for a moment than to live in eternal ignorance."*

Satyavrat had embraced this philosophy with absolute devotion. He saw the world in black and white—truth and falsehood, right and wrong. Yet, as he grew, he saw the suffering that came from truth wielded without mercy. He questioned, but he never strayed.

And now, he stood in the middle of a grand hall, a thousand eyes upon him. The weight of judgment pressed upon his chest like an iron chain. Before him knelt a trembling child, no older than ten, clutching his mother's robes. The mother's face was pale, her lips trembling, her body shaking like a leaf caught in a storm. *"He did not steal,"* she pleaded, her voice raw with desperation. *"He is innocent! Please, my lord, he is just a child!"*

Tears streamed down her face, her hands clasped in supplication. The boy, his eyes wide with terror, clung to her as if she were the only thing keeping him from being swallowed by the void. *"I was hungry,"* the boy whispered, barely audible. *"I just wanted to help my mother."*

Satyavrat's breath hitched. He could see the truth as clearly as the midday sun. The child had taken the bread—his hands still bore the faint scent of it. The law was clear, the truth undeniable. And yet, as he gazed upon the boy, skin stretched thin over frail bones, he felt something deeper than truth—he felt torment. He felt the unbearable weight of justice without mercy.

The mother's sobs filled the hall, echoing against the stone walls. She clutched her son tighter, her body wracked with despair. *"Please!" she cried, her voice breaking. "He is just a child! Have mercy!"*

The boy whimpered, his tiny hands trembling as they clung to her robes. His wide, terrified eyes met Satyavrat's, searching for hope, for salvation. *"I was hungry,"* he *whispered. "I just wanted to help my mother."*

One of the guards stepped forward, his grip firm on his spear. *"You must decide, O Seer of Truth,"* he intoned, his voice *devoid of emotion. "What does the truth demand?"*

Satyavrat's breath hitched. The weight of judgment pressed upon him. The truth was undeniable—but was truth alone enough?

But Satyavrat saw the truth. The child's hands still bore the scent of stolen bread. A truth undeniable. A truth that burned.

"The truth must be spoken," he said, his voice steady, yet his soul *trembled. His father's teachings echoed in his mind—truth above all else, truth as the only path. But now, standing before the weeping mother and the frightened child, another voice whispered within him—was truth without compassion still truth?*

He clenched his fists, battling the storm in his heart. *"The law is clear,"* he repeated, *but the words felt heavier, burdened with doubt. The boy's terrified eyes bore into him, pleading for mercy where there was none. The mother's cries felt like knives, cutting through his conviction.*

Vishnu's voice surrounded him, neither condemning nor forgiving. *"What is truth, Satyavrat, if it breaks rather than mends? What is justice if it does not heal?" "Truth is a blade, Satyavrat. But must it always cut? Can truth be justice if it leaves only suffering?"* His voice did not just question—it awakened. *Like a ripple through the still waters of Satyavrat's convictions, it revealed the unseen fractures between righteousness and cruelty. The hall grew still, even time seemed to listen.*

Vishnu's voice echoed around him.

As the guards reached for the child, Satyavrat's breath caught. Could he wield truth without it becoming a weapon?

Anirvan: The Curse of Fearlessness

Anirvan had been raised in a family of warriors, where fear was seen as the greatest enemy. His father, a hardened general, had drilled into him since childhood that fear was a disease, a poison that weakened the soul. *"Fear is an illusion,"* his father would say, his voice sharp as steel. *"Only the weak succumb to it. The strong conquer it before it even takes root."*

"Pain is temporary, but fear lingers if you let it," his father would continue, pacing before him after every battle drill. *"A man who fears is already half-defeated. Would you rather live a coward or die with honor?"*

Anirvan, bruised and exhausted, would lift his chin. *"I will not fear, Father. Never."*

His father would nod approvingly. *"Then you are ready to lead, my son. Remember, a warrior who flinches is a warrior who falls."*

As a boy, Anirvan had been thrown into brutal trials—left alone in the wild with no food or water for days, forced to survive in the freezing mountains where wolves roamed, made to stand in a pit of snakes until he no longer flinched. He had been sent into battle before he could even hold a sword properly, beaten down by warriors twice his size, his wounds left untreated to teach him endurance. Each time he had survived, not because he was the strongest, but because he had trained his mind to banish fear before it could take hold. *"Pain is a test,"* *his father had said as Anirvan bled on the cold ground. "Fear is a choice. And you, my son, shall never choose it."*

A storm raged around Anirvan, yet he stood unmoving, unyielding. He had always been fearless. Fear was the weakness of the wavering mind, and he had conquered it.

"Fear is the enemy," he told himself. "It is a shadow, cast by doubt. I have walked through darkness without trembling. I have faced death without faltering. I am not afraid."

Yet a whisper in his mind fought back. But what if you should be?

Anirvan was known across the lands for his fearlessness. Warriors admired him, kings sought his counsel, and enemies despised him. But those who hated him most wished to break the legend of his unshaken spirit. And so, they devised the cruelest test.

One fateful evening, his enemies struck where it hurt most. They captured his younger brother—his life, his heart, the one person he had sworn to protect above all else. His brother was not just his kin; he was his anchor, his closest friend, the laughter in his darkest days. Anirvan had always thought himself untouchable, but now, as he stood before the horrific sight, something inside him cracked.

His brother, hands bound, a dagger pressed against his throat, trembled but did not cry. The shadowy figure looming behind him sneered. *"You fear nothing," the figure mocked. "Then let us see if you fear loss."*

"Anirvan!" his brother gasped, his voice strained but desperate. His small frame trembled, his wide, innocent eyes searching Anirvan's face for reassurance. "Brother, please! You always protect me... you said you would never let anything happen to me! Don't let them— don't let them take me away!"

"Silence!" the enemy barked, pressing the blade closer, drawing a thin line of blood. "Tell me, fearless warrior, does your heart race? Does your mind waver? Or will you stand still as we carve his life away?"

The enemy's sneer deepened. *"But I'll give you a choice, oh fearless one. Show me fear—beg, weep, tremble before me—and I will spare your brother's life. Prove that you are human, that you are not made of stone, and I will release him. Or..." he dragged the blade agonizingly slow along the boy's throat, "...watch him die, knowing his last breath was spent crying out for the brother who never flinched."*

Anirvan's breath hitched. His chest tightened. His brother whimpered, eyes wide with terror. *"Anirvan, please!"* he *choked, his voice quivering. "You always said you'd protect me. You said nothing could hurt us if we were together!"*

Tears welled in the boy's eyes, his small body shaking against the cruel grip of their captors. *"Brother, don't just stand there!"* he pleaded. *"Please! Just say something—just make them stop! I don't want to die, Anirvan!"*

The enemy pressed the blade deeper, drawing more blood. *"Look at him, Anirvan,"* he sneered. *"So innocent. So helpless. And you? So fearless? Or are you?"*

Anirvan's breath grew ragged, his fists trembling. His brother's voice cracked with desperation. *"Brother, please! Just this once, let them see you care! Let them see you feel!"*

His enemies laughed, circling like vultures. *"Well, fearless warrior? Will you kneel for him? Will you let the world see that even you can break?"*

Anirvan's fists clenched, his nails digging into his palms. His entire life, he had been taught that fear was an illusion, a weakness to be eradicated. But now, staring at his brother's terrified face, fear was not an illusion. It was real. It was suffocating. His chest heaved as an unfamiliar weight crushed his ribs, a foreign tremor creeping into his fingers. His mind screamed at him to act, to remain unshaken, but his heart bled at the sight before him.

"No," he thought desperately. *"I do not fear. I cannot fear."*

But his brother's sobs shattered his resolve.

"Brother, please!" his voice broke, raw with agony. *"Don't let them do this! You always said you would protect me! Was it all a lie?"*

The enemy sneered, pressing the blade deeper against the boy's throat. *"Do you hear him, fearless one? He is begging for his life. And yet, you stand frozen like a statue. What kind of protector are you?"*

Anirvan's breath hitched, his soul tearing apart. For the first time in his life, he was afraid—not for himself, but for what he was about to lose. Fear twisted through him, choking him with its merciless grip. His lips parted, but no words came. His mind raged, but his body would not move.

And then, a voice in the wind—Brahma's voice—cut through the storm in his heart.

"You have walked without fear, Anirvan. But without fear, have you ever truly valued what you protect?"

Brahma's voice echoed in the winds, ancient and knowing. *"You have walked without fear, Anirvan. But without fear, have you ever truly valued what you protect?" And with that echo came the scent of creation itself—of beginnings long past and futures yet unnamed. Anirvan stood not in fear, but in realization—that perhaps fear was not a weakness, but a compass pointing to what he held sacred.*

For the first time in his life, Anirvan trembled.

Vidyatman: The Chains of the Past

Vidyatman had been born into a family of scholars, generations of wisdom flowing through his veins. His father, a revered teacher, had instilled in him the belief that knowledge was the highest form of power. From an early age, Vidyatman could recall details from the past with uncanny clarity, his mind a vast ocean of memories not only of his own life but of those who had come before him.

"Wisdom is both a gift and a curse," his father had often said. "To know the past is to understand the world, but to be burdened by it is to be shackled by ghosts. Imagine a man who remembers every betrayal, every war, every loss—does he not live in perpetual sorrow? And yet, without memory, would we not be doomed to repeat those very mistakes?"

Vidyatman had once asked, *"Then what is the purpose of wisdom, Father, if it only brings pain? If the past cannot be changed, then why must we remember it? Do our memories serve us, or do they chain us? And if knowledge is power, why does it feel like a burden?"*

His father had smiled, placing a hand on his head. *"The purpose of wisdom, my son, is to guide—not to control. The river remembers every stone it has touched, but it does not stop flowing. Learn from the past, but do not let it drown you. A man who carries the past like chains will never move forward, but one who carries it as a lantern will light the way for others."*

He continued, *"The world is built upon stories of those who came before us. You must ask yourself—do you seek wisdom to find truth, or to change fate? There is a difference, my son. If you tamper with what has been, you risk unraveling the very essence of karma. Knowledge is power, but power without purpose is destruction."*

Vidyatman's eyes flickered with doubt. *"But what if the past is full of mistakes? What if I see pain that could have been avoided? Should I not act?"*

His father's voice softened. *"Would you play the weaver and undo the very fabric of time? And if you change another's fate, do you not steal their right to learn, to grow, to choose? True wisdom, Vidyatman, is knowing when to intervene—and when to let destiny take its course."*

Visions swirled around Vidyatman—faces of the past, lives lost, mistakes repeated. He had always believed knowledge was power. Yet, now, as he watched history unfold again and again, he saw something else—a cycle, unbroken, unrelenting. Shadows of fallen warriors, betrayed rulers, lost children, and shattered dreams filled his sight. Each face, each story whispered of choices made and regrets left behind.

He gasped as he saw a man he once admired—a wise king—make the same error that had doomed his lineage. He saw a mother, blinded by vengeance, set into motion events that would cost her the very child she sought to protect. His breath hitched as he recognized the pain, the longing, the hope that flickered before each disaster. Could they not see? Could they not learn?

"If I can see the past," he murmured, his voice shaking, "then why do we keep making the same mistakes? Why must the same sorrows echo through time?"

The answer lay before him. A woman, once a ruler, now fallen, betrayed by those she trusted. He had seen it before, in countless stories. He could warn her, stop it from happening. His heart pounded as he clenched his fists, torn between duty and impulse. Would altering her fate be an act of wisdom or arrogance? Would he be saving her, or merely postponing an inevitable lesson?

"I could change this," he whispered to himself. "I could spare her the pain. I could rewrite this story. But at what cost?"

Doubt gnawed at him. If he interfered, would he be any different from those who sought control over destiny? And if he walked away, was he condemning her to suffer needlessly? The battle raged within him, the weight of his gift pressing down on his soul.

And then, the voice of Vishnu echoed in his mind: *"Would you rewrite the past, Vidyatman, and risk unraveling the very thread of karma? Will you decide for others what pain they must endure, what lessons they must learn? Or will you trust the order of the universe to guide them, as it has guided you?"*

But Vishnu's voice whispered, firm yet compassionate. *"If you change the past, do you strip others of their right to choose? Can fate be rewritten without unraveling free will? Would you mend a broken thread only to risk unraveling the entire fabric? The past carries pain, yes, but also wisdom. Would you deny others the growth that comes from their trials?"*

His hands trembled. Knowledge was power—but was power always meant to be used? If he did not use it, was he wasting the gift bestowed upon him? If he did, was he overstepping the bounds of destiny? *"Then what will I do with this power?"* he whispered, his voice heavy with the weight of choice. *"Is it meant to guide or to control? To heal or to destroy?"*?

"If I can see the past," he murmured, *"then why do we keep making the same mistakes?"*

The answer lay before him. A woman, once a ruler, now fallen, betrayed by those she trusted. He had seen it before, in countless stories. He could warn her, stop it from happening.

But Vishnu's voice whispered. *"If you change the past, do you strip others of their right to choose? Can fate be rewritten without unraveling free will?"*

Vidyatman clenched his fists. Knowledge was power—but was power always meant to be used?

Karunesh: The Keeper of Kindness

Karunesh, the Hand of Compassion, was born into a lineage of healers, where kindness was both a duty and a legacy. His father, a revered physician, was known not only for his medical skills but for the wisdom with which he dispensed them. *"A healer does not just cure,"* he would say, placing a reassuring hand on young Karunesh's shoulder. *"We mend bodies, yes, but true healing is of the soul. Teach a man to*

*endure his pain, and he will rise stronger. Ease his suffering too
soon, and he may never learn resilience."*

From an early age, Karunesh roamed the crowded lanes
of their village, following his father's footsteps into
homes thick with incense and despair. He saw wounds
that no salve could heal—grief in a mother's eyes as she
wept over her stillborn child, rage in a soldier's heart as
he cursed his failing limbs. He heard their pleas, their
cries for relief, and wondered—was it enough to mend
the body while leaving the heart untouched?

As he grew, he honed his skills, his hands becoming as
steady as his father's. Yet, doubt gnawed at him. Healing
was meant to ease pain, but what if pain had its own
purpose? What if suffering was not merely an affliction
but a teacher? Could mercy, when granted too freely,
become cruelty in disguise?

One fateful evening, he encountered an old man writhing
in agony, begging for relief. Karunesh raised his hands to
heal him, but his father stopped him. *"Let him bear it a little
longer,"* his father murmured. *"Watch, my son."*

Hours passed. The old man endured, his body wracked
with agony, his breath coming in ragged gasps. Karunesh
watched, torn between his instinct to heal and his
father's command to wait. The old man's fingers clawed
at the dirt, his cries echoing in the still night. But then,
something shifted. His trembling ceased, his eyes, though
bloodshot, held an eerie calm. With a final, steady breath,

he whispered, *"I have conquered my suffering. I do not fear it anymore."*

And then, silence. His body slumped, lifeless.

Karunesh stood frozen, horror coursing through him. *"Father... what have we done? Why did we let him suffer only to die?"*

His father's gaze was firm but sorrowful. *"At times, mercy is not in healing, but in letting go. Sometimes, the dead are freed in a way the living never can be."*

Karunesh's heart pounded. He had spent his life believing in healing, in relief. But now he saw the weight of mercy, the unbearable choice between saving and surrendering. His hands trembled as he clenched them into fists.

"Then what is my power for? If I can ease suffering, how can I stand by and let it persist? How do I decide who is to endure and who is to be freed? Am I playing god? Or am I simply refusing to accept fate?"

His father placed a firm hand on his shoulder. *"That is the burden of a true healer, my son. The hardest lesson is knowing when to heal... and when to let go."*

Karunesh could not sleep that night. The old man's final breath echoed in his mind. His fingers ached, longing to reverse what had been done. But could he? Should he? He sat in the dim light, staring at his hands. Hands meant to heal. Hands meant to comfort. Yet, tonight, they had done nothing.

"What if I had acted? Would he still be alive? Or would I have robbed him of his final lesson?"

He clenched his fists. *"Is healing always the right answer? Is suffering always the enemy? Can I truly wield this power if I do not understand its cost?"*

The questions haunted him, twisting like vines around his heart. He wanted to ask his father again, to demand an answer that would silence the turmoil within him. But he already knew—some answers could not be given. They had to be found.

When the gods granted him the power to erase suffering, he saw it as a blessing. Yet, his trial revealed its curse. He was confronted with a village stricken by plague. He had the power to heal them, but as soon as he did, another plague would come, and another, endlessly. A divine voice whispered, *"Will you ease suffering endlessly, or will you teach them to endure and grow?"*

His heart ached as he watched a child grasp his fingers, pleading, *"Save us."*

His father's voice echoed in his mind: *"Karunesh, to truly help, one must know when to let go."*

Tears welled in his eyes. *"Then what will I do with this power? If healing never ends, am I merely delaying the inevitable? Can I truly stop suffering, or will it always find a way?"*

The gods now directly questioned him, forcing him to confront the true nature of his power.

"You have seen the weight of your gift," Vishnu spoke. "What will you do with it now?"

Karunesh's voice trembled. *"I don't know. If healing is endless, then suffering is endless too. If pain returns in another form, am I only a fleeting relief? Am I fighting a war I cannot win?"*

Shiva's voice rumbled, deep and unshaken. *"Not every battle is won by victory. Some are won by wisdom. Will you choose to wield your power blindly, or will you learn when to step back?"*

Karunesh closed his eyes, his heart heavy. *"I always thought healing was the greatest act of kindness. But now I see… kindness is sometimes letting go."*

The gods watched in silence, and for the first time, Karunesh felt the true burden of his power.

Yuktashakti: The Burden of Sight

Yuktashakti, the Weaver of Fate, was born to a lineage of mystics, her parents revered for their insight into the unseen. Her mother, Vasundhara, was known for her wisdom and patience, while her father, Maharishi Dhiratman, was a seer who had glimpsed the very fabric of time. They raised her in solitude, away from the distractions of the world, training her mind to perceive the delicate threads of destiny weaving together.

"Power is responsibility, my child," her mother would often remind her. "To hold knowledge is to bear its weight with care. Wisdom without restraint is a storm without direction. And remember, the stars may illuminate the night, but they do not command the dawn.

Choose your words carefully, for even the whisper of fate can stir the winds of destiny."

Her father, ever solemn, would warn, *"To see is not to change. To know is not to act. The moment you interfere, you may weave chaos into fate. The river does not halt its course for the stone that falls within it, but the ripples reach farther than the eye perceives. Be wary, my child—sometimes, in trying to mend the weave, one may unravel it entirely."*

From a young age, she felt the burden of her gift— visions of futures yet to unfold, paths unwritten but destined. She was taught that her power was not to be wielded recklessly but to be understood. Yet deep in her heart, a question lingered: If she could see the inevitable, was it truly inevitable?

The first time her power revealed itself, she had been just a child, no older than ten. One evening, as she sat beside the village fire, her mind was suddenly flooded with a vision—a beloved elder collapsing, his final breath slipping away beneath the same banyan tree where he often shared stories of the past. Panic seized her tiny frame, but she knew she had to act. She ran to him, breathless, pleading, *"You must not go near the banyan tree tonight! Please, something terrible will happen."*

The elder, startled by her urgency, hesitated, then chose to heed her warning. He turned away from the tree, choosing another path home. But fate was cruel. A sudden storm brewed, lightning cracking through the sky. As he hurried, he slipped on the wet stones, tumbling down the ravine that lined the village. By the time help arrived, it was too late.

Yuktashakti stood frozen, staring at his lifeless form, horror clutching her heart. Her breath came in ragged gasps, her hands trembling as she reached out but dared not touch him. "No... *no, this wasn't supposed to happen,"* she whispered, her voice breaking. *"I was trying to save you... I was trying to help."*

Her knees buckled beneath her as grief overtook her. Tears streamed down her face as she clutched her head. *"Why? Why did this happen? I changed the path, I warned him! It wasn't meant to end this way!"*

Her vision swam with unshed tears, her mind reeling. She clenched her fists, her nails digging into her palms. *"If I cannot change fate, then why am I cursed to see it? If all paths lead to suffering, then what is the purpose of my gift?"* Her voice cracked, a sob tearing through her. *"Am I nothing more than fate's cruel spectator? A puppet who watches the play but cannot move?"*

Her mother's voice echoed in her mind—Power is responsibility. Her father's warning loomed over her—To see is not to change. But what was the point of seeing if she could do nothing? What was the point of knowing if all she did was make things worse?

She let out a choked sob, turning her tear-streaked face to the heavens. *"What kind of power is this if I can't even save one life? If I am doomed to watch, helpless, as suffering unfolds? Am I nothing but a seer of sorrow, cursed to witness agony and call it fate? If every path leads to loss, then tell me—why was I given these eyes to see but not the hands to change?"*

That day, she learned a painful truth—knowledge alone did not grant control, and fate would not be defied so easily. No matter how desperately she fought, no matter how fiercely she screamed against the heavens, the universe remained indifferent. And worst of all, she was powerless to undo what had been done. The weight of her gift became a shackle, a cruel joke played by destiny itself, leaving her to drown in the torment of knowing, yet never changing.

Years passed, and her power grew sharper. She could see the fabric of fate as clearly as others saw the stars in the night sky. Kingdoms fell, lovers parted, destinies fractured—and she saw it all before it happened. But knowledge had become her tormentor, for every vision brought a choice. If she spoke, did she alter fate? If she remained silent, did she condemn?

One day, a woman stood before her, tears in her eyes, desperation clawing at her voice. *"Tell me, will my child survive?"* Her hands trembled as she clutched Yuktashakti's robes, her breath ragged with grief.

Yuktashakti swallowed hard, her own heart twisting. *"If I tell you, will you live in fear, clinging to hope that is already unraveling? Or will you fight against the tide, only to find yourself drowning in its wake?"*

The woman's lip quivered. Her breath hitched as she clutched her chest. *"My son is my life, my heartbeat.*

If anything happens to him, I will die! I will do anything to save him—anything!"

Yuktashakti hesitated. A vision bloomed in her mind—a sickly child gasping for breath, his mother's tears soaking the sheets. She saw the mother rushing to the herbalist, bringing remedies too late. Her cries pierced through the night, raw and desperate, but fate remained unmoved. And then, she saw the child's funeral pyre burning beneath the watchful moon, the mother's anguished screams swallowed by the crackling flames.

"I... I cannot say," she whispered, her voice breaking.

"You won't, or you can't?" the woman cried, her nails digging into Yuktashakti's skin. *"If you know, how can you stay silent? How can you stand there, knowing my child's fate, and say nothing? Are you a goddess playing with mortal lives, or a coward too afraid to speak the truth?"*

Tears welled in Yuktashakti's eyes as she wrenched herself away. *"Because I don't know what is worse—telling you and giving you false hope or staying silent and letting you grieve before the storm comes."*

The woman collapsed to her knees, sobbing. Yuktashakti turned away, guilt pressing against her ribs like an iron cage. She clutched her chest, feeling the ache of countless moments where she had been forced to bear witness, unable to intervene. Memories of pleading eyes, of desperate cries, of hands reaching toward her, hoping she could bend fate to their will, surged through her mind.

"Is knowing enough if I cannot act?" she whispered, her voice breaking. *"What good is sight if all I can do is watch suffering unfold? If my knowledge brings nothing but helplessness?"* Her breath trembled as she looked up at the vast, indifferent sky. *"Am I cursed to be nothing more than a witness to pain?"*

A gust of wind rustled the trees, whispering through the void of her despair. Somewhere in the distance, thunder rumbled, as if fate itself were answering her grief.

She was the Weaver of Fate, but was she its master? Or merely another thread, bound by the very destiny she sought to unravel?

Nirvansh: The Sage of Mastery Over Desire

Nirvansh, the Sage of Mastery Over Desire, was not always a being of supreme wisdom. Before the gods chose him, he was Vasujit—a man born with an extraordinary burden and an even greater gift. From the moment of his birth, he was different. His eyes, deep and unyielding, seemed to hold the weight of knowledge far beyond his years. As a newborn, he did not wail like other infants; instead, he gazed at those around him, as if already understanding their deepest desires.

Even as a child, he could sense the weight of unspoken desires in those around him. When his father bartered in the market, Vasujit could feel the silent greed clinging to the merchants like an invisible mist. When his mother prayed, he could hear the yearning behind her words—the aching wish for something beyond mere devotion. Unlike others who learned of longing through experience, Vasujit was born knowing. He did not need to be told what a person craved—he felt it, like a whisper in his bones. The world wore its desires like chains, and he alone could see them gleaming in the unseen light.

Unlike others who were enslaved by their longings, Vasujit saw them. He did not need to be told what a person craved—he felt it, like a whisper in his bones. It was not a blessing. It was a curse.

As he grew, the gift became a torment. He could not escape the pull of others' desires. In a crowded room, it overwhelmed him—the hunger for wealth, the thirst for power, the ache of unfulfilled love. Each longing was a wave crashing against his mind, relentless and inescapable. He tried to ignore it, tried to pretend he was like everyone else, but the truth gnawed at him. Why was he the only one who could see this force so clearly? Why did no one else understand the chains they had forged around themselves?

He would watch men laugh while their souls whispered of sorrow. He would see mothers cradle their children while their hearts yearned for something more. He would listen to the prayers of sages, and within their words of renunciation, he could hear the silent clamor for recognition. *"What is this endless hunger that consumes the world?"* he would wonder. *"Is there no one free from its grasp?"*

One day, when the weight of it all became unbearable, he stood before the mirror, staring into his own haunted eyes. *"Am I too bound by these invisible chains?"* he whispered, his voice barely audible over the storm raging within him. *"Do I suffer the same affliction as those around me? Am I, too, just another soul shackled by longing?"*

He clenched his fists, his breath unsteady. *"Or... am I meant to break free? To rise above this endless hunger that devours the world? And if so—how?"*

The silence of the room offered no answers, but deep within, a flicker of something stirred—a defiance, a question, a path yet unseen.

One evening, he confronted his father, Shaurya, as the merchant counted his coins under the golden glow of the lantern. Vasujit had watched him for years, watched the way his fingers traced the edges of each coin with reverence, as if touching something sacred. There was a time when Vasujit believed the same—when he thought gold was the answer to every question, the solution to every fear. But now, he felt nothing but emptiness in its presence.

"Father," he said, his voice steady yet laced with an unfamiliar weight, *"do you ever feel... truly free? Free from this endless pursuit, free from the hunger that never fades?"*

Shaurya chuckled, his eyes never leaving the shimmering pile before him. He ran his fingers through the coins, letting them slip through his hands like grains of sand, relishing the metallic clink. *"Freedom? My son, gold is freedom. Gold bends the will of men, opens the doors that remain shut, and silences the mouths that dare to oppose. With enough of it, even fate bows. What is freedom if not the power to shape the world as you wish?"*

Vasujit frowned, his chest tightening. He leaned forward, his voice sharper now, almost desperate. *"Then why do you never have enough of it, Father? If gold is freedom, why do you still count it every night as if it might disappear? Why does your hunger for it only grow? If wealth truly grants control, then why does it control you?"*

His father's hands stilled, the flickering lamplight casting shadows across his weathered face. For the first time, he looked up, meeting his son's gaze with an expression Vasujit could not decipher. There was confusion there, perhaps even fear.

Shaurya's fingers tightened around a gold coin, his knuckles whitening as he held it up to the lantern's glow. His eyes gleamed with an almost feverish intensity. *"Because, my son,"* he said, his voice low and unyielding, *"to stop wanting is to stop living. What is a man without ambition? Without hunger? Without the fire to claim what should be his? A fool, a beggar—nothing."*

Vasujit stared at him, the weight of those words sinking into his soul like stones into water. He wanted to protest, to argue that life should be more than this endless hunger. But instead, he turned and walked away, his heart heavy with the truth he wished he could unsee.

Vasujit left without another word, his heart heavy. He turned to his mother, Anindita, hoping for answers. She knelt in prayer, her lips moving in silent devotion.

"Mother," he whispered, kneeling beside her. *"What do you ask for when you pray?"*

She opened her eyes, startled, as if awakened from a distant dream. A flicker of uncertainty passed through her gaze before she whispered, *"Peace." Her voice was soft, yet laced with an unspoken weight, as if the very word carried a burden too heavy to release. She lowered her eyes, clasping her hands together, her fingers trembling slightly. "I pray for peace, my son, but some desires are like shadows. No matter how much light you seek, they linger."*

Vasujit tilted his head. *"And have you found it?"*

She hesitated. Her fingers clenched slightly against the folds of her prayer shawl, the tremor in them barely perceptible. A deep sigh lifted her shoulders, but she did not exhale fully, as if the very air held the weight of her unspoken thoughts. Her gaze flickered to the flickering lamp before the deity, lingering on the flame as though seeking an answer from the divine. The silence stretched between them, thick and laden with emotions she could not—perhaps would not—express. Then, slowly, her hands tightened together in prayer once more, her knuckles pale against the strain.

That night, Vasujit sat under the stars, alone with his thoughts. He clenched his fists, trying to silence the endless murmurs of longing that filled his mind. *"Why am I cursed to see this?"* he whispered. *"Why must I feel the desires of others as if they are my own?"*

A voice within him answered, a voice not his own but something deeper, something ancient. Because you were not meant to be ruled by desire. You were meant to master it.

Years passed, and Vasujit sought answers in every path he could. He traveled to distant lands, debated with scholars, meditated in solitude, but nothing freed him from the burden. He indulged in every pleasure, thinking that if he experienced desire fully, it would release him. It did not. He renounced all pleasure, thinking that if he denied it completely, it would disappear. It did not. The more he fought it, the stronger it became.

Then came the moment of transformation—the night that defined his destiny.

A devastating storm swept through his homeland, washing away the homes and wealth his family had built. Merchants who once bowed to his father turned their backs; sages who once praised his mother's devotion now spoke of fate's cruelty. Vasujit wandered through the wreckage, watching as people clung to their possessions even as the floodwaters claimed them. A man wailed as his golden chest was swallowed by the tide, a woman clutched shattered bangles to her chest, whispering prayers for their return. In the faces of the desperate, Vasujit saw suffering—not in the loss of wealth, but in the refusal to let go.

He stepped forward and spoke, his voice cutting through the chaos.

"Why do you weep for that which was never truly yours?" he asked.

An elder turned to him, his eyes filled with anguish. *"Without our treasures, who are we?"*

Vasujit met his gaze, realization dawning. *"You are not what you own. You are what you become when all is taken away."*

In that moment, enlightenment struck him. Desire was not the enemy—it was attachment that enslaved. It was not longing that caused suffering, but the inability to release what one could not hold forever. He closed his eyes, the weight of countless desires pressing upon him, yet for the first time, they did not consume him. He whispered to the storm, as if speaking to his own soul:

"What is it that I have chased all my life? Was it power? Love? Or merely the illusion of control?"

The winds howled in response, carrying his voice into the void. His heart ached with the truth he had ignored for so long.

"I sought to master the world, but the world was never mine to hold. I longed to possess, but what I truly needed was to understand."

As he knelt before the rising waters, a divine voice resonated through the storm. Vishnu himself appeared, his form radiant, his presence both serene and boundless.

"You have glimpsed the truth," Vishnu declared. *"Desire is neither shackles nor wings—it is the current that moves all souls. Master it, and you shall guide the new world."*

Vasujit bowed, his heart steady. *"Then teach me, my Lord."*

With that, he was reborn as Nirvansh—the one who transcends longing. No longer torn between indulgence and denial, he emerged as a beacon of balance. He did not preach renunciation, nor did he encourage reckless pursuit. Instead, he revealed the path of mastery: to desire with awareness, to strive without enslavement, and to walk the world without being bound by it.

Sitting beneath the vast expanse of the twilight sky, Nirvansh closed his eyes, feeling the pulse of the universe around him. He spoke softly to himself, as if voicing the wisdom that had taken lifetimes to understand. *"The heart will always yearn, but it is the mind that must learn to guide it. Should a river curse its flow, or should it carve its way with grace?"*

A disciple nearby, watching his master in silent reverence, gathered the courage to ask, *"Master, do you never feel the pull of desires anymore? Do you not miss the passions of your past?"*

Nirvansh smiled, his gaze steady. *"To feel desire is to be alive. But I no longer serve it—I make it serve me. Passion is a fire; left untamed, it consumes. But when mastered, it illuminates the path."*

As Karma Yug dawned, Nirvansh became the teacher of kings and seekers alike. He guided rulers to lead without greed, lovers to cherish without possession, and sages to seek without losing themselves. He walked through the new world, teaching that true liberation was not in denial, but in wisdom. His words became the foundation upon which Karma Yug would rise, for only those who mastered their desires could shape the destiny of this new era.

One evening, a disciple asked, *"Master, do you never long for anything?"*

Nirvansh smiled. *"To long is to live. But to be free is to choose which longing to follow."*

Thus, the Sage of Mastery Over Desire walked forth, not as one who had abandoned the world, but as one who had mastered its greatest force—turning longing into light, and desire into destiny.

As the trials ended, the Seven Sages found themselves once again standing in the void between realms. The weight of their own choices still lingered in their souls, their minds echoing with the voices of their past, their fears, and the burdens they had long carried.

The gods, watching in silent judgment, now stepped forward. Brahma, Vishnu, and Shiva—creation, preservation, and destruction—stood before them, their celestial forms glowing with an energy that pulsed through the very fabric of existence.

Brahma, the Creator, spoke first. His voice was both gentle and unyielding. *"You have walked through the fires of your own doubts, yet the embers of uncertainty still flicker within you. You question yourselves, your choices, your very worth. But tell me, is a river lesser for not knowing where it leads? Is the dawn weaker because it has not yet seen the day?"*

Vishnu's gaze swept across the sages, piercing through their silence. *"Each of you was chosen not for your perfection, but for your struggles. Rudrayan, you wield justice, yet tremble before mercy. Satyavrat, you uphold truth, yet waver when it wounds. Anirvan, you have conquered fear, yet now stand shaken by loss. Vidyatman, you carry wisdom, yet wonder if it is a curse. Karunesh, you heal, yet fear that suffering is beyond your power. Yuktashakti, you see fate, yet question if you are its prisoner. And Nirvansh, you have mastered desire, yet find yourself haunted by its shadow."*

Shiva's voice rumbled through the void, a force of both destruction and revelation. *"Karma Yug is not a gift—it is a battle yet to be fought. The old ways will resist you. The ghosts of the past will whisper in your ears. The world you are meant to shape will not surrender willingly to your vision. And so, we ask you once more: will you forge this era, or will you be consumed by the weight of your own doubts?"*

The gods fell silent, waiting. The Seven Sages stood at the precipice of destiny, their hearts pounding with the echoes of their trials.

The choice was now theirs.

Would they rise?

Or would they fall, as so many before them had?

Their answers would shape the world to come.

Karma Yug had begun.

And so, the echoes of their trials lingered not in judgment, but as hymns of awakening.

Each soul marked not by flaw, but by the fire that endured it.

The heavens did not decree their worth—their choices did.

In the silence after divine verdicts, the sages did not seek answers—they became them.

The Karma Yug dawned not with celebration, but with a whisper...

A whisper that said, *"Walk, for the path will reveal itself to those who dare to choose."*

"The stars did not sing. The gods did not cheer.

Only silence greeted the birth of a new era—

A silence heavy with the weight of choice.

They were not perfect. They were not divine.

But they had walked through their own darkness

And dared to carry light.

From justice tempered by mercy, From truth softened by love,

From fear unraveled by loss, From wisdom that chose silence,

From healing that knew surrender, From sight that bore restraint,

From desire that learned to bow—

Rose not heroes,

But the humble hands of fate. And so began Karma Yug,

Not with the roar of gods, But with the quiet breath of seven souls

Who rose because they fell, And chose because they broke.

Let the old world end, Let the new one rise.

Not on power, But on the ashes of pain

Made sacred by understanding."

Chapter 4

The Burden of Free Will

The sages had conquered their doubts, emerged from their trials, and now stood on the precipice of a new beginning. The celestial decree had been spoken—there would be no divine intervention, no predetermined righteousness, no ordained destiny. Only karma would govern this world. Each action, each choice, would shape the fate of mortals. Yet, as they descended upon the ruined earth, their hearts filled with the weight of their purpose, they were met not with gratitude, but with resistance.

The people, still shackled by the past, recoiled at the thought of a world where justice was not handed down from above but carved by their own deeds. Fear clouded their eyes, their minds clinging to the stories they had known for generations—of gods who punished and rewarded, of fate that unfolded like a divine script, of cycles that turned predictably, ensuring that the wicked would fall and the righteous would rise. Now, those stories were gone, replaced by a truth they were unwilling to accept.

A restless murmur spread through the gathered survivors, voices rising in fragmented protests. A man with sunken eyes and a voice hardened by suffering stepped forward, his frustration barely restrained. *"Why you seven?"* he demanded, his gaze shifting from one sage to another. *"Why not two? Why not three? If the gods have forsaken us, why do we need sages at all?"* A woman, her arms wrapped protectively around a frail child, added, *"What makes you different from us? Are we to blindly follow yet another group claiming to hold wisdom? What gives you the right to decide the course of this new world?"* Others joined in, their doubts spilling forth like a long-contained flood. *"Are you chosen by the gods, or is this just another cycle of power?"* *"Seven of you, but why? What meaning does that number hold?"* *"If we are to shape our own fates, why should we look to you?"* The crowd shifted uneasily, torn between distrust and desperation. They had lost faith in divine intervention, yet the idea of navigating this broken world alone was just as terrifying. Their eyes searched the sages for answers, for justification, for something—anything—that would make sense of the uncertainty consuming them.

"This cannot be," an elder muttered, his voice thick with disbelief as he gripped his wooden staff. His aged hands trembled. *"The gods test us. They must! They would not abandon their children to chaos."*

A woman, her cheeks hollow from hunger, her eyes weary from endless prayers that had gone unanswered, shook her head. *"And what if they have? What if this is all that is left? If there is no Satya Yuga, no divine justice, then who will protect the weak? Who will decide what is good and what is evil?"*

A murmur of unrest spread through the gathering. Their faith had already been shaken by the silence of the gods. Now, it threatened to shatter entirely. Some clung desperately to old rituals, believing that if they prayed hard enough, if they repented long enough, the gods would be moved to restore order. Others, however, stood at the edge of something new—something terrifying yet undeniable.

One of the sages, Dharmisth, the Sage of Righteous Balance, stepped forward. His deep-set eyes bore no trace of anger, only understanding. *"You seek the gods to tell you what is right,"* he said, his voice steady. *"But tell me, when a mother shields her child from harm, does she do so because she fears divine punishment, or because her heart compels her to protect what she loves?"*

The people hesitated. A young man, his arms crossed tightly over his chest, frowned. *"She does it because it is right,"* he admitted.

Dharmisth nodded. *"And who decided it was right?"*

The young man opened his mouth, but no words came. A flicker of realization passed through the crowd, but resistance remained.

Samyak, the Sage of Absolute Truth, stepped forward next. *"You say the gods have abandoned you. But ask yourselves this—if a farmer tills his land and plants no seed, will the earth still give him grain?"*

"No," someone muttered.

"And if a man stands at the edge of a river, waiting for the gods to carry him across, will the water part for him?"

Silence.

Samyak's gaze swept over them, piercing through their doubt. *"Then why do you wait for the gods to hand you a fate you must create yourselves?"*

The people shifted uneasily. A man, his face lined with the struggles of survival, spat on the ground. *"Easy for you to say! You are sages—you have power, wisdom. But we? We are nothing! We are weak, lost. How can we shape our own fate when we do not even know where to begin?"*

Bodhidhar, the Sage of Eternal Awareness, spoke then, his voice like a whisper carried by the wind. *"The weakest man can still choose to rise. The lost can still choose to walk forward. That is the power of karma. It does not ask for strength, only for action."*

"But what if we fail?" a woman asked, her voice barely above a breath. *"What if we make the wrong choices?"*

Satvavrat, the Sage of Purity and Will, smiled, a rare expression of warmth. *"Then you will learn. And you will rise again."* He gestured to the ruins around them. *"Look at this land. It has been broken by war, by greed, by time itself. But do you think this is the end of it?"*

The people hesitated. Slowly, heads shook.

"This land will bloom again," Satvavrat continued. *"Not because the gods will make it so, but because we will plant the seeds, tend the soil, nurture its growth. The same is true for this world. Karma Yug is not an age that will be gifted to you. It is an age you must build."*

The weight of his words settled over the crowd, but uncertainty still lingered. Nirvansh, the Sage of Mastery Over Desire, watched them for a long moment before stepping forward, his voice carrying an edge of quiet authority. *"You fear a world without gods,"* he said. *"But tell me, when you suffered in the past, when your prayers went unanswered, did you not still rise each morning and fight to survive? When the divine silence stretched over your grief, did you not still hold your children close and move forward?"*

The woman who had spoken before blinked, her throat tightening. *"I… I did."*

Nirvansh nodded. *"Then you have always known the truth. The gods were never your saviors. You were your own salvation."*

A deep hush settled over the people. Some looked away, unwilling to accept the truth just yet. Others lowered their heads in thought.

Kratu, the Sage of Creative Destruction, took a step forward, his presence commanding. *"We do not ask you to believe in this all at once,"* he said. *"We do not demand that you abandon your fears in a day. But know this—whether you accept it or not, the world has already changed. Karma Yug has begun."*

He turned, looking at his fellow sages, and each of them nodded.

"We will guide you," Chaitanya, the Sage of Conscious Action, said, his voice calm yet firm. *"Not as rulers. Not as lawgivers. But as those who have walked through fire and emerged with the*

knowledge that no god, no prophecy, no fate will ever shape this world again. Only karma. Only action."

The crowd stood in stillness, absorbing the weight of this new reality. Some still held onto the past, clinging to prayers that would never be answered. But others—those who had already suffered the harshest truths of life—felt something stir deep within them. A spark. A choice.

The sages had spoken. The gods had fallen silent. The new age had begun.

The sky above stretched in an endless expanse of muted gray, a vast canvas smeared with the remnants of ash and despair. Below, the earth lay cracked and barren, its once-fertile lands now a graveyard of civilization. Broken pillars of temples, half-buried under dust, whispered forgotten prayers to gods who had long since fallen silent. The wind carried the faint echoes of a world that had crumbled under the weight of its own greed and arrogance.

Scattered across this wasteland were the remnants of humanity—hollow-eyed figures draped in rags, their backs hunched under an invisible burden. Some sat in clusters around dying fires, their hands stretching towards the last warmth they could find. Others trudged through the ruins like restless spirits, searching for something—anything—that could restore the world they once knew.

When the sages arrived, their radiant forms stark against the desolation, the people recoiled. Not in reverence, but in suspicion.

"Where are the gods?" a voice, raw with age and grief, broke the silence. An elder, his skeletal frame trembling under the weight of time, stepped forward. "Why have they forsaken us? Why do they not mend what has been broken?"

Another voice rose from the gathering—a younger man, his face gaunt but his eyes burning with defiance.

"We have waited for Satya Yuga! We have prayed! We have sacrificed! And yet, the gods do not come!" His fingers curled into fists, his fury barely contained. "Now you speak of karma, of choice? What choice do the cursed have? We are already doomed!"

The murmurs of the crowd swelled, a tide of fear and frustration threatening to crash over the sages. They had not come to rule, yet they now stood before a people desperate for salvation—whether by gods or by conquerors. And in that moment, the sages understood: teaching Karma Yug would not be as simple as speaking truths. It would demand something far greater—a way to guide those who had forgotten how to walk on their own.

The air was thick with the scent of decay, a vile mixture of scorched earth, rotting carcasses, and the acrid stench of abandoned cities. The remnants of Kalyug still festered in the land, an unhealed wound pulsing with the echoes of past horrors. The sky, once blackened by war and greed, now hung in a lifeless gray, neither promising rebirth nor condemning further ruin. The wind moaned through the ruins, carrying the whispers of the dead, their voices merging with the murmurs of the living who clung to the edge of existence.

The survivors, frail and hollow-eyed, emerged like shadows from the wreckage, their skin stretched thin over bones that had known hunger for too long. They huddled together, staring at the sages with expressions carved from equal parts fear and defiance. Some gripped rusted weapons—daggers and makeshift spears, remnants of a war that had long since ended, yet still ruled their minds. Others clutched at broken idols, their trembling hands seeking solace in gods who no longer answered.

To them, the idea of a world without gods, without fate, was unfathomable. It was as though the last pillar of their reality had been shattered, leaving behind only an abyss of uncertainty. Without divine intervention, who would punish the wicked? Who would bless the righteous? The gods had been their shield and their chains—without them, they were free, but freedom was terrifying. And so, as they looked upon the sages, it was not awe or reverence that filled their gaze—it was suspicion, resentment, and a desperate, lingering hope that perhaps, just perhaps, the sages could give them the answers the gods had denied them.

The murmurs in the crowd grew louder, voices intertwining in confusion, rage, and frustration.

"Who are they?" a woman whispered, clutching a child to her chest. "Are they gods in disguise? Have they come to judge us?"

"They wear no crowns, carry no weapons," an older man muttered, his fingers tracing the beads of a prayer mala. "And yet, they stand as though the world bends to their will."

"Why have they come now?" another demanded, stepping forward with trembling fists. *"Where were they when our homes burned? Where were they when our children starved?"*

"Where is God?" a young boy called out, his voice small but piercing. *"Has He abandoned us? When will Satya Yuga begin? Will we ever be free of this suffering?"*

Another voice, cracked with age, joined in. *"If karma is to decide our fate, then why were we born into ruin while others lived in glory? Is this justice? And why Karma Yug? We waited for Satya Yuga, we prayed for deliverance! Was our faith in vain? What makes Karma Yug necessary? What is its purpose?"*

A woman, clutching a frail child to her chest, sobbed. *"If the gods do not return, who will protect us? Are we to be forgotten like the dust beneath our feet?"*

A man, his face etched with bitterness, shouted, *"You speak of choice, but what choice do the cursed have? If karma governs all, then why do tyrants feast while the righteous starve?"*

The murmurs swelled, growing into a storm of voices, each demanding answers that had long eluded them. *"What if we refuse to accept this Karma Yug?"* one man challenged, stepping forward. *"What if we demand that the gods return? What if we make them hear us?"*

The air around them grew heavy, a sea of broken souls looking to the sages for salvation, for a truth that would not shatter them further.

"Why Karma Yug?" a man roared, his voice thick with anger. *"We have suffered through Kalyug, we have endured torment*

and destruction! We waited for Satya Yuga! We were promised salvation, not another age of struggle!"

A woman, her face twisted with grief, cried out, "You say karma will rule us now? What does that mean? Will the weak still be trampled? Will the powerful still feast upon the helpless?"

"Explain to us!" another demanded. "What is Karma Yug? If the gods have forsaken us, if dharma will no longer guide us, then what rules are we to follow?"

"We have prayed, we have bled, we have begged for mercy!" an elder shouted, his voice breaking. "If Satya Yuga will never come, then why should we accept this fate? Why should we trust you?"

A younger man, his eyes burning with desperation, pushed forward. *"If karma is now our judge, then where is justice? Where is fairness? Why do some suffer from birth while others are born into wealth and power? Tell us, wise ones! Answer us!"*

A hush fell over the gathering as their eyes locked onto the sages, demanding answers that had been lost to time. Their desperation was raw, their longing unbearable. The weight of centuries of suffering clung to their words, pressing upon the sages like an unseen force.

The sages exchanged glances, each feeling the burden of those unspoken prayers, the cries of those who had waited too long for salvation. The weight of desperation clung to the air, thick and suffocating. Some among the crowd fell to their knees, pleading with trembling voices.

"Tell us what we must do!" cried a woman with hollowed cheeks, clutching at the hem of her tattered sari. *"Give us a sign that we are not forgotten."*

An elder, his voice raw with grief, wailed, *"Have we not suffered enough? What debt do we still owe?"* A man, younger but hardened by loss, stepped forward, his hands clenched into fists. *"If the gods have forsaken us, why should we listen to you? How do we know you are not here to mislead us further?"*

A sudden hush fell over the gathering as a child, no older than seven, stepped hesitantly toward the sages. His ribs jutted out beneath his dirt-streaked skin, his wide eyes filled with something deeper than fear—hope. *"If the gods are inside us,"* he whispered, *"then why do I feel so empty?"*

"Where are the gods?" a voice called from the gathering crowd, an elder with a face lined by time and suffering. *"Why do they not restore our lands, heal our wounds? Have we not suffered enough?"*

"We have waited for Satya Yuga," another voice joined in, anger lacing its words. *"And yet, it does not come. Instead, you speak of karma, of choice. How can we choose when fate has already cursed us?"*

They had come to guide, not rule—but how could they teach a world that refused to listen? The people were not just resistant; they were desperate, clinging to the remnants of a faith that had long abandoned them. Their fury was not just at the sages but at the cruel silence of the gods they had worshipped for centuries. Their questions were not mere inquiries but accusations, demands for justice against an existence that seemed to mock them.

A man stepped forward, his face twisted with anguish. *"You come to us now, when all is lost? Where were you when our cities burned? When our children died in our arms? Are we to trust your words when the gods themselves have turned away?"*

A woman, her voice hoarse with grief, pointed at the ruins around them. *"What guidance can you offer when we have nothing left? Are you here to tell us that our suffering is our own doing? That we deserve this?"*

A young warrior, his body scarred from battles that had yielded nothing, spat at the ground before them. *"If this is Karma Yug, then tell me—what karma did the newborns commit to be born into a world of dust and death? What justice is this?"*

The sages remained silent, absorbing the weight of the pain before them. This was not merely a world without faith—it was a world betrayed by it. To rebuild, they would have to teach these people how to believe in something greater than divine rescue. They would have to teach them to believe in themselves.

A Fractured People

At first, the people resisted. The idea of a world without Satya Yuga, without the return of an age of truth and divine order, was unthinkable. They had been raised on stories of cycles, of the inevitable descent of ages, followed by the cleansing dawn of righteousness. Now, that promise had been shattered. The gods had spoken—the cycle was broken. But how could mortals accept that they were now their own salvation?

At first, they raged. *"This is a test,"* *the elders murmured among themselves. "A punishment. The gods wish to see if we are worthy of Satya Yuga. If we pray harder, if we fast, if we offer more, surely they will return." Yet the heavens remained silent. No divine voices, no miracles, no signs. The world stood still in the eerie quiet of its new reality.*

Then came the bargaining. *"Perhaps we must perform a great yagna,"* a priest suggested, his voice feverish with desperation. *"We must cleanse ourselves, rid our souls of the last traces of Kalyug's sins." Fires were lit, chants filled the air, and sacrifices were made. But the skies did not part. The gods did not answer.*

Slowly, fear turned into quiet acceptance—not because they truly believed, but because they had no choice. Hunger gnawed at their bellies, and the sun continued to rise and fall, indifferent to their suffering. One by one, they began to approach the sages, hesitantly, warily. At first, they asked in whispers.

"Is it true?" a woman with hollowed cheeks and tired eyes asked. "That Satya Yuga will never come?"

A sage, his robes worn by time, simply nodded.

A man, his hands calloused from years of labor, clenched his fists. *"Then what do we do? If there is no Satya Yuga, how do we live?"*

Another spoke, his voice cracking, *"Without the gods to judge us, who will tell us what is right? Who will decide what is just?"*

The sages listened. They did not force answers upon those who came, nor did they command obedience.

Instead, they let the questions settle, let the people hear their own voices echo in the emptiness left behind by their lost faith.

One night, a youth—his face marked with the soot of a dying fire—stood before them, his eyes brimming with defiance. *"You say the gods are within us. But men are selfish. They lie, they kill, they betray. If there is no divine law to guide us, won't we become worse than before?"*

A sage, older than the rest, looked at him and said, *"Then tell me—why are you here? Why do you seek our counsel, if men are nothing but liars and betrayers?"*

The youth faltered. His lips pressed together, his breathing shallow. *"Because… I want to do what is right."*

The sage smiled. *"And there is your answer."*

The crowd murmured, uneasy. Some nodded, understanding flickering in their eyes, while others still clung to the shadows of the past. They were not yet ready to accept this new world, not fully. But still, they came.

Not because they believed, but because for the first time, they had to seek answers not from the heavens, but from within themselves.

In the ruins of an ancient temple, a council of survivors had gathered. The once-grand pillars, now crumbling and covered in vines, bore witness to their whispered fears and quiet rage. The flickering light of oil lamps cast long shadows across the shattered stone floors, illuminating faces etched with suffering and distrust.

Among them were remnants of once-powerful rulers, their fine robes reduced to tattered cloth, their authority now only a memory. Priests who had once led grand rituals to gods who no longer answered clutched their sacred texts, their faith shaken but not abandoned. Warriors who no longer had a war to fight sat with their weapons resting beside them, their restless hands tightening into fists as they searched for an enemy to blame.

They spoke in hushed yet urgent tones, their voices thick with uncertainty, anger, and longing. *"These sages claim to bring wisdom, but what wisdom can they offer in a world abandoned by the divine?"* a former king muttered, his once-proud posture now slumped with exhaustion.

"They seek to strip us of our faith," one priest argued, his voice rising. *"If the gods are silent, then we must pray louder. We must offer more, sacrifice more. Have we not always been tested? Perhaps this is another trial!"*

A warrior, his arms still bearing the scars of old battles, scoffed. *"Tested? By whom? By what? The gods have left us to rot! And now these sages expect us to rule ourselves? No man is fit to bear such responsibility."*

"If karma truly rules this world," another man said, his voice bitter, *"then why are the wicked still alive while the innocent perish? Should we not take power into our own hands? Should we not demand the justice the gods have denied us?"*

The sages knew they had little time before chaos erupted. The council was a fragile thing, held together by fading hope and rising desperation. If they did not act soon, the people would either fall into lawlessness or create a new tyranny under a false sense of divine justice.

"They seek to strip us of our faith," one priest argued. "If the gods are silent, then we must pray louder. We must offer more, sacrifice more."

"The gods have abandoned us," countered a former king, his robes now tattered but his arrogance intact. "And now these sages expect us to rule ourselves? No man is fit to bear such responsibility. What wisdom can they offer that the gods could not?"

A merchant, his once-golden bangles now rusted, scoffed. *"They come to speak of karma, but what karma brought ruin upon our lands? What karma allows tyrants to rise while the innocent fall?"*

A grieving mother clutched a bundle of cloth, her voice choked with sorrow. *"If karma is the answer, then why was my child taken before he had a chance to even act? What justice is there in an infant's suffering? Tell me, sages!"*

A young warrior, anger flashing in his eyes, stepped forward. *"You speak of a new age, but what of those who only knew the old? What if we refuse this Karma Yug? What if we choose to forge our own fate, not one dictated by unseen forces?"*

A warrior, his arms still bearing the scars of old battles, stood. *"If karma truly rules this world, then the strong will rise and the weak will perish. That is nature's law."*

The sages knew they had little time before chaos erupted. If they did not act, the people would either fall into lawlessness or create a new tyranny under a false sense of divine justice.

The Sages' Struggle

Each sage faced their own battle within this turmoil, each burdened with the weight of their past trials and the immense responsibility that now lay upon them. As the people cried out for answers, their voices filled with rage and sorrow, the sages felt the invisible chains of expectation tightening around them. Could they truly guide a broken world without becoming its rulers? Could they teach mortals to embrace Karma Yug when they themselves were still grasping its vastness?

Rudrayan, the Hammer of Justice, struggled with whether to impose order or allow people to find their own way. If he enforced laws, was he not acting as a ruler? The weight of justice pressed heavily upon him, a burden he had carried long before the gods had chosen him. His soul was forged in the fires of judgment, his hands steady in delivering fairness where cruelty reigned. But now, standing before a world in ruins, he saw that justice was no longer a simple measure of right and wrong—it was tangled in desperation, in grief, in the unyielding need for survival.

He watched as the people clashed, their voices raw with pain, their fists raised in anger. *"We need laws! We need protection!" some cried. Others raged, "No more rulers! No more masters! We will not bow again!" The weight of their words bore into him, echoing the same dilemmas that had haunted him in his past. Justice was meant to balance the world, but what if the world rejected balance? What if they demanded chaos over order? If he did nothing, suffering would continue unchecked. If he imposed rule, he would become the very thing he once fought against.*

His hands clenched at his sides, the ghostly weight of his war mace pressing against his palm. Was justice a guiding light, or was it a chain? Could it exist without power? Without force? He had once believed that righteousness alone was enough, but now, as he gazed upon the fractured souls before him, he realized justice meant nothing if those who needed it did not accept it. And so, his greatest trial began—not in battle, but in restraint, in the delicate act of giving justice without becoming a tyrant.

Satyavrat, the Bearer of Truth, found himself torn— should he reveal that the gods had deliberately stepped back, or would that knowledge break the spirits of those clinging to faith? The burden of truth weighed upon him like an unrelenting storm, pressing down on his chest with every cry of despair that rose from the people. He had always believed truth to be the highest virtue, a force that could illuminate even the darkest of paths. But now, as he stood amidst the ruins of a civilization that had lost everything, he questioned whether truth was a healer or a destroyer.

The people were desperate, their faith hanging by a thread. Their eyes, hollow with suffering, searched for something—anything—that could make sense of their anguish. If he told them the gods had abandoned their role as protectors, would they find freedom in that knowledge, or would it push them deeper into the abyss of hopelessness? Would it shatter the last fragments of their belief, leaving them lost in a world where neither gods nor destiny offered guidance?

He felt his breath grow unsteady as his mind raced. He had spent lifetimes seeking and speaking truth, but for the first time, he feared its consequences. What if the truth did not set them free? What if it left them untethered, drowning in their own uncertainty? His heart pounded as the questions clawed at him, demanding an answer he did not yet have. He clenched his fists, his nails biting into his palms. Was he ready to bear the burden of breaking the very faith that had sustained these people through their darkest days?

He looked around at his fellow sages, seeking solace in their presence, but the answer was his alone to find. The truth was a blade—sharp, unyielding, and dangerous in the wrong hands. And as he stood before a world on the edge of collapse, Satyavrat knew that how he wielded it now would determine whether he became a savior or an executioner.

Anirvan, the Flame of Courage, sought to inspire action, but many were too afraid to embrace change. He stood among them, his heart a roaring inferno of passion and frustration, yet all he saw before him were faces drained of hope, bodies too weary to rise. He had led warriors into battle, faced death without flinching, but never had he encountered a battle like this—one against fear itself.

His gaze swept across the people, searching for even a flicker of defiance, some ember of resistance that could be fanned into a flame. But their eyes held only exhaustion, their voices hollow with defeat. *"What courage do we have left?"* one man murmured, *his fingers tracing the scars that lined his arms. "We have fought, we have lost. We have nothing more to give."*

A woman clutched her child tightly, shaking her head. *"You ask us to fight, but for what? The gods have forsaken us, the land is barren. We have no homes, no food, no strength. Tell me, warrior—can courage fill the stomachs of our starving children?"*

Anirvan's fists clenched, his breath unsteady. He had never doubted his own resolve, had never questioned the fire within him. But as he stood amidst these broken souls, he felt a terrifying chill—the possibility that perhaps, for the first time, courage alone was not enough. If a warrior had no army, if a leader had no followers, did his fire mean anything at all? He could not force them to rise, could not command their hearts to burn with the same unrelenting passion that lived within him. He had to show them, make them believe that courage was not the absence of fear, but the act of moving forward despite it.

But how does one breathe life into the spirit of the defeated? How does one teach the lost to find their own way? Anirvan had spent a lifetime defying fate, but now, as the weight of their despair threatened to smother his flame, he wondered—was this a battle even he could win?

Vidyatman, the Keeper of Knowledge, watched mortals twist karma into an excuse for selfishness, and a deep sorrow settled in his heart. He had once believed knowledge to be the purest of gifts, a guiding light that illuminated the righteous path. But now, as he observed the world he had sworn to help rebuild, he saw knowledge being used not as a tool for growth, but as a weapon for deception.

He had hoped that with the gods stepping back, mortals would rise to their own potential, taking responsibility for their actions and forging a path based on wisdom. But instead, they had manipulated karma into justification for their misdeeds. The rich claimed their wealth was a result of past virtues, absolving themselves of any duty to aid the suffering. The cruel declared that their victims must have wronged the cosmos in a past life, twisting the very essence of karma into a shield for their atrocities. Vidyatman watched as the cycle of ignorance continued, and the weight of it pressed upon his soul like an unbearable burden.

Doubt gnawed at him. Had they failed? Had the sages, in their vision for a just world, unleashed something far worse—a society where knowledge no longer guided but excused? His breath grew unsteady as he wrestled with the thought. Was wisdom meant to be given freely, or was it something that had to be earned? Should he speak, correct the misguided, and impose truth upon those who refused to seek it? Or was this the test of Karma Yug itself—that the world must stumble and fall before it could truly learn?

The frustration of it all burned within him. He had believed that humanity, when freed from the cycle of divine intervention, would reach for greatness. Instead, they grasped at shadows, distorting truth to serve their desires. And so he stood, watching a world that both needed him and rejected him, unsure whether his duty was to guide or to let them break against the weight of their own choices.

Nirvansh, the Master of Desire, saw mortals clinging to greed, lust, and old ambitions, and a deep sadness settled within him. He had believed that Karma Yug would grant them the wisdom to understand desire—not to shun it, not to indulge in it blindly, but to master it. Yet before him was a world that had learned nothing. The desperate clung to wealth, the broken sought pleasure to drown their sorrow, and the powerful tightened their grip on all they could hoard. He had thought desire could be tempered, but now it raged unchecked, consuming those it touched.

He watched as men quarreled over scraps, their hunger turning them into animals. He saw rulers demanding tributes, as if their titles still held meaning in a world reduced to ruin. He heard whispered bargains, promises exchanged in dark corners, mortals willing to trade their very souls for the illusion of control. The sight of it filled him with a quiet devastation. Had they, the sages, not come to break these chains? Had they not vowed to lead humanity into an age where desire no longer ruled the heart, but was ruled by it?

His throat tightened with an ache he did not expect. He had wanted to believe in them. He had wanted to believe that given the choice, mortals would rise above their impulses, that they would seek balance. But looking at them now, he felt as though he had lost something— some faith in the very beings he had sworn to guide. If this was the world they had chosen, then what was left for him to teach? His purpose felt fragile, slipping between his fingers like sand. Perhaps the fire of desire could never be tamed. Perhaps it would always burn too brightly, too wildly, reducing everything in its path to ash.

Karunesh, the Vessel of Mercy, felt his soul weighed down by the unbearable burden of his purpose. He had always believed that kindness could mend the deepest wounds, that compassion could soften even the hardest hearts. But as he stood amidst the ruins of a broken world, he found himself questioning everything he had ever known. Mercy had become a foreign concept in a land where survival was all that mattered, where men turned on each other like starving beasts and kindness was mistaken for weakness.

He saw mothers who had lost their children, eyes hollowed out by sorrow so profound that no amount of comfort could reach them. He watched the strong trample the weak, justifying their cruelty with the law of survival. Those who still believed in mercy were mocked, their open hands slapped away, their generosity taken as foolishness. And Karunesh, once a beacon of selfless love, now stood paralyzed by a sorrow he did not know how to bear.

His chest ached with the weight of helplessness. What was the purpose of mercy in a world that no longer wanted it? What use was kindness when people saw it as nothing more than a tool to be exploited? He had given his heart freely, and now it felt shattered, each jagged piece a reminder of the love he had offered and the pain he had received in return. If compassion had no place in Karma Yug, then what place was there for him?

For the first time, Karunesh feared that mercy had become obsolete, and with it, so had he.

Yuktashakti, the Weaver of Fate, stood apart from the others, her gaze heavy with sorrow as she watched mortals twist the essence of karma into something unrecognizable. She had spent lifetimes weaving destinies, guiding the flow of existence, but now, she found herself unraveling. The threads of fate, once intricate and purposeful, now lay frayed and chaotic in her hands. Would they ever truly understand it? Or was she trying to weave meaning into a world that refused to see the pattern?

She had believed that with the gods stepping back, humanity would embrace the power of karma, take control of their own destinies, and rise to something greater. But instead, they feared it. They blamed karma for their suffering, clung to old beliefs, and sought to escape the burden of choice. Some declared it a cruel force, punishing them for sins they did not remember. Others used it as an excuse to do nothing, surrendering to their misfortunes as if they had no agency over their lives. She saw the confusion in their eyes, the refusal to accept that karma was not a punishment nor a reward, but a mirror. And yet, they refused to look.

A deep weariness settled in her bones. If mortals would not take responsibility for their own fates, then what was the purpose of Karma Yug? Had they, the sages, merely cast humanity adrift, tearing away the illusion of divine control only to leave them lost in an endless sea of uncertainty? The thought left a hollow ache within her. She had been so certain, so unwavering in her belief that the world was ready. But now, as she watched them flounder, she could not help but wonder—had they been wrong? Had she been wrong?

The feeling of loss crept upon her, sharp and unforgiving. She was the Weaver of Fate, yet she had never felt so powerless. The fabric of the world had changed, and for the first time, she questioned whether she could still shape it—or if the tapestry of existence was unraveling beyond repair.

For days, the Seven Sages watched in silence as the people wandered like lost souls, their eyes filled with unanswered questions, their voices heavy with doubt. The ruins of the past stood around them—temples once grand now reduced to fractured stone, rivers that had once carried sacred chants now flowing sluggish and murky. The world had changed, and yet the hearts of mortals still clung to an old promise, a cycle that would never return. Satya Yuga was gone. The gods had stepped back. And now, the people stood at the precipice of an unknown age, desperate for guidance.

One evening, as the last embers of the sun bled into the sky, turning the horizon into a vast sea of fire and ash, the Seven Sages gathered on the highest plateau overlooking what remained of the land. The wind howled around them, carrying whispers of prayers that had gone unanswered, of faith teetering on the edge of despair.

"It is time," said Nirvansh, the Sage of Mastery Over Desire, his deep voice laced with an understanding that went beyond mere wisdom. "They do not yet understand what it means to shape their own fate. They still search the skies, waiting for a sign that will never come."

"Because for lifetimes, they have been told that salvation is something given, not earned," replied Samyak, the Sage of Absolute Truth. His piercing gaze swept across the land, his mind tracing the turmoil in the hearts of the people. "Even now, they hope for a decree, a command, a law handed down from a divine voice. But no such voice will come. We must be the ones to guide them."

"We must be careful," interjected Dharmisth, the Sage of Righteous Balance, his expression thoughtful. "It is not for us to replace the gods. We cannot dictate the laws of Karma Yug—we can only show them how to walk the path. If we impose order as the gods once did, we will be no different from the past, and this new age will become nothing but another cycle waiting to collapse."

A moment of silence followed, heavy with the weight of their responsibility.

"But they are not ready," said Satvavrat, the Sage of Purity and Will. "Left to their own devices, some will falter, some will fall into chaos. They do not yet know how to navigate a world where karma is their only judge. We must prepare them. Not as rulers, not as lawgivers, but as guides."

They knew words alone could not teach what a lived truth could. And so, an idea began to form—of trials not imposed, but observed. Of lessons not preached, but lived. A way to let the people discover, through consequence, what the gods had chosen to let go unspoken.

"They already come to us," said Bodhidhar, the Sage of Eternal Awareness. His eyes, filled with an ancient knowing, reflected the flickering torches below where people gathered in huddled circles, speaking in hushed tones. "Every day, they seek our wisdom, asking how they must live, how they must decide. We cannot ignore them. Whether we accept it or not, they need us."

"But will they accept Karma Yug?" questioned Chaitanya, the Sage of Conscious Action. "They still long for a savior. If we show them a path too unfamiliar, too uncertain, they may reject it and spiral into madness. Change is never accepted easily."

"Then we do not tell them to follow," said Nirvansh, his voice steady. "We show them what it means to live by karma. They do not need words—they need to see the power of their own choices, the consequence of action, the responsibility that comes with free will. They must witness Karma Yug, not be forced into it."

The final sage, Kratu, the Sage of Creative Destruction, exhaled deeply, his gaze fixed upon the distant ruins. *"We will teach them,"* he murmured. *"Not through rules, not through fear, but through wisdom. Through example. If they come seeking justice, we show them fairness. If they come seeking purpose, we show them the weight of their actions. If they come seeking power, we show them restraint. And if they come seeking the gods, we show them their own reflection."*

A hush fell over them as the wind shifted, carrying the scent of earth and smoke. In the valley below, the people continued to murmur, their uncertainty weaving into the night like a restless spirit.

Nirvansh stepped forward, his robes billowing as he extended his hands to his brothers. *"Then it is decided,"* he said, his voice resonating with finality. *"We do not turn them away. We do not let them slip into ruin. From this day forward, we stand as the first guides of Karma Yug. Not as rulers, not as gods—but as those who have seen beyond the illusions of fate. We will show them that their choices are their prayers, their actions are their offerings, and their deeds alone will shape the world to come."*

One by one, the sages clasped their hands together, their souls bound by the oath they had taken. A new dawn was rising, not just in the sky, but in the hearts of those who stood below, waiting for a sign that they, too, could rise beyond what had been and embrace what could be.

And so, the first age of Karma Yug began—not with divine decree, not with miracles, but with the quiet resolve of seven sages who chose to stand beside mankind, not above them.

The First Trial of Karma Yug

The sages stood before the people, their faces lined with the weight of their purpose. They had not come to offer salvation, nor to dictate laws. They had come to awaken a truth that had been buried beneath centuries of dependency. The gods had stepped away, not in abandonment, but in trust. And yet, the people saw this as betrayal, as punishment. The sages knew this battle was not of flesh and steel, but of the mind—of breaking the chains of expectation that had bound mortals to the illusion of fate.

And so the sages, each bearing a fragment of truth, stepped forth—not to silence the people, but to reflect their own doubts and answers back at them.

Rudrayan's voice was steady, yet heavy with the burden of justice. *"You ask why Karma Yug has come instead of Satya Yuga. You ask why the gods do not return. The answer is before you. Look around at what has become of the world after Kalyug. You longed for Satya Yuga, yet you continued the cycle of greed, war, and suffering. The gods could not bring forth Satya Yuga when mortals themselves had made the world unworthy of it."*

Satyavrat stepped forward, his eyes piercing into the crowd. *"You ask for truth, but can you bear it? You seek justice, but do you wish it only for yourselves? The gods did not forsake you. They gave you what you always lacked—the right to choose, the power to forge your own destiny. Do not seek divine hands to mold your fate. Your karma shall shape the world now. And if you refuse this, if you turn away from Karma Yug, then know this: you will not suffer because the gods are absent. You will suffer because you have denied yourselves the strength to stand."*

Anirvan, the fire in his voice unrelenting, raised his hands toward the people. *"Courage is not waiting for salvation. It is stepping forward even when there is no path. You cry out for gods to save you, but have you saved yourselves? When you see injustice, do you fight it? When you see suffering, do you ease it? If you wish to reject Karma Yug, then tell me, what will you do instead? Will you wait again, pray again, and blame the heavens for what you refuse to change?"*

Vidyatman let out a breath, his sorrow evident. *"Knowledge is the light that should guide you, yet you choose to walk in darkness. You twist karma to suit your own desires, using it as an excuse for cruelty or inaction. But karma does not bend to your whims. It is neither a weapon nor a shield. It is the weight of your deeds, and in Karma Yug, no gods will bear that weight for you. If you refuse to understand this, then you will fall not because the gods have left, but because you have abandoned wisdom."*

Nirvansh's voice was quiet but firm. *"Desire is not your enemy, but your master if left unchecked. In Kalyug, mortals let greed, ambition, and indulgence consume them. Now, in Karma Yug, you have the choice—to master desire or be enslaved by it. If you reject this age, then you choose to remain shackled to the same hunger that destroyed your world."*

Karunesh's face, filled with sorrow, scanned the crowd. *"Compassion is what makes you human, and yet I see you forsaking it. The weak are abandoned, the grieving left unheard, and mercy mistaken for foolishness. You demand justice, but do you grant it? You seek kindness, but do you offer it? Karma Yug will not punish you, nor will it save you. It will reflect what you choose to become. Will you be better? Or will you continue to destroy what little remains of your world?"*

Yuktashakti, her voice woven with finality, took a step forward. *"The threads of fate no longer belong to the gods. They are in your hands. If you reject Karma Yug, you reject the power to weave your own destiny. But know this—there is no going back. If you wait for gods to return and shape your world, you will wait for eternity. If you refuse to act, the world will not stop for you. Karma Yug is here, and whether you accept it or not, it will move forward. The only question that remains is whether you will move with it."*

The sages stood in silence, their words hanging in the air like the final toll of a great bell. The people, their voices once raised in fury and despair, now stood quiet, their minds churning with the weight of truth. The choice had always been theirs. Now, they could no longer deny it.

But words, even those spoken with wisdom, could only reach so far. The sages realized that true understanding would not bloom through speech—it needed soil, action, and consequence.

Recognizing the people's unwillingness to accept responsibility, the sages devised a trial—a challenge that would force mortals to face their own choices.

They would create a scenario where survival depended not on divine intervention, but on understanding karma's true nature.

A village, once prosperous, lay in ruins. Its wells had dried, its fields were barren. Nearby, a rival group hoarded food and water, refusing to share. The sages declared:

"You are free to act. If you take by force, you will face the consequences. If you negotiate, you may find a path forward. If you choose neither, you will suffer the weight of inaction. Choose wisely, for karma does not forget."

The people hesitated. Some sought diplomacy, others prepared for war. A few chose to wait, hoping for a divine answer that would never come. And thus, the first test of Karma Yug began.

Ending: The Dawn of True Choice

As events unfolded, the sages did not intervene, only watched. Some choices led to suffering, others to wisdom. A group of desperate villagers, instead of negotiating, stormed the food reserves of a neighboring settlement, killing many in the process. Days later, a sickness spread through their stolen grain, leaving their own people weak and dying. In another village, a leader who sought power under the guise of justice began executing those he deemed 'unworthy' of survival. Within weeks, his own followers turned on him, consumed by the very fear he had instilled.

Elsewhere, a merchant manipulated karma's teachings to hoard wealth, claiming his prosperity was his divine right. But when famine struck, the very people he had oppressed rose against him, reducing his riches to ashes. A grieving mother, unable to accept the loss of her child, blamed karma itself and refused to move forward. Her sorrow hardened into bitterness, pushing away all who once cared for her, until she was left in solitude. And in the midst of all this, a young warrior, convinced that strength alone defined destiny, chose conquest over peace. He waged war on a weaker settlement, only to be struck down by a child who had learned to wield his own fate.

But among these tragedies, there were those who saw Karma Yug for what it was. A farmer, left with nothing, shared his last morsel with a starving stranger. That stranger, in turn, led him to fertile lands beyond the ruined cities, where they began anew. A woman, once betrayed, chose to forgive rather than seek revenge, and in doing so, mended the broken bonds of her people. A scholar, ridiculed for his beliefs, continued to teach the ways of karma, planting the seeds of understanding that would one day bloom into wisdom.

For the first time, mortals realized that their fate was their own.

The air was thick with the scent of charred wood and damp earth, remnants of a world that had collapsed under the weight of its own sins. The sky, once a canvas of endless blue, remained a dull, ashen gray, reluctant to shed its grief.

Among the ruins, a child stood barefoot on the blackened ground, his small fingers clutching the torn edges of a cloth wrapped around his frail frame. His hollow eyes, reflecting both wonder and fear, darted between the shadows of the past and the uncertain dawn stretching before him. He had seen temples crumble, rivers dry up, and stars flicker into darkness. He had heard his elders whisper that the gods had turned their backs, that divinity had abandoned them.

Yet now, something stirred in the silence.

He hesitated before stepping forward, his tiny feet sinking into the damp soil. With a quivering breath, he approached one of the sages standing at the edge of the ruins—a figure draped in flowing robes, his face carved with the wisdom of lifetimes. The sage's eyes, deep as the cosmos, held no sorrow, no anger—only an unshakable stillness.

The child's voice, barely more than a whisper, broke the hush of the morning.

"Will the gods ever return?" His words wavered, laced with the desperate hope of someone too young to understand loss but old enough to fear it.

The sage turned his gaze toward the horizon, where the first light of dawn struggled to break through the shroud of despair. For a long moment, he said nothing, allowing the weight of the question to settle in the air. Then, with a gentleness that carried both comfort and truth, he placed a weathered hand upon the boy's tangled hair.

"The gods never left," he murmured, his voice steady as the earth beneath them. *"They are within every choice you make."*

The child's brows furrowed, his small hands tightening into fists. *"But… I don't see them,"* he whispered, his voice trembling. *"I prayed when my mother was taken by the sickness. I begged when my father disappeared into the storm. I called out to them when I was alone in the dark."* His throat tightened as he looked up at the sage, his eyes brimming with unshed tears. *"No one answered."*

The sage kneeled before him, the weight of lifetimes resting in his gaze. *"Did you survive?"* he asked gently.

The child hesitated. *"Yes…"*

"Did you find the strength to wake up every morning?"

The boy swallowed and nodded.

"And did you choose to keep walking, even when there was nothing ahead but shadows?"

A single tear slipped down the child's cheek as he whispered, *"I did."*

The sage smiled, pressing a warm palm against the boy's chest, right over his heart. *"Then tell me, child—who was it that kept you going?"*

The boy's lips parted, but no answer came. His heartbeat pounded beneath the sage's hand, steady and strong.

"You looked for the gods in the sky," the sage continued, his voice like the whispering wind. "But they were never there. They were in your every breath, your every step, your every choice to fight, to survive, to hope."

The child let out a shaky breath, his gaze lowering to his own hands, small and trembling. *"Then… I am not alone?"*

The sage's fingers curled slightly against the boy's chest. *"Not as long as you remember that divinity is not something you wait for. It is something you live."*

The sun climbed higher, its golden light washing over the ruins, turning the blackened earth to gold. The child lifted his face, allowing the warmth to touch his skin, and for the first time in a long time, he did not shiver.

And as the dawn of Karma Yug unfolded before them, he took his first step into a world where fate was no longer written in the stars, but in the hands of those who dared to shape it.

And as the sun continued to rise, painting the world anew, the first true day of Karma Yug began.

And so the stars remained silent, not out of indifference, but reverence.

For in the stillness of the heavens, the song of free will had begun.

No divine hand would turn the page, no god would author their fate.

It was theirs now—each word written in the ink of choice, each line forged by consequence.

And though the gods no longer walked beside them,

They had gifted mortals something far greater than miracles—

The power to shape a world not foretold, but forged.

The burden of free will was heavy.

But in that weight, there was wonder.

In that struggle, there was hope.

And in every breath that rose to meet the dawn, Karma Yug was born again.

Chapter 5

The New Order

Defining the Laws of Karma Yug

A cold wind swept over Vishwadhara, the sacred plateau where the Seven Sages stood, their cloaks billowing like the banners of an age long past. Below them, th e remnants of humanity gathered—broken rulers, wandering warriors, orphaned children, and forgotten scholars. They had no gods to pray to anymore. No fate to bind them. Only their own choices.

The land beneath the plateau was scarred—charred remains of once-great cities stretched into the horizon, rivers ran dark with the remnants of fallen empires, and the earth itself seemed to sigh under the weight of its own suffering. The last echoes of Kalyug still lingered in the air—a world once consumed by greed, war, and blind faith had collapsed, leaving only uncertainty in its wake.

Yet in that uncertainty, there was hope. Hope that from the ashes of the past, a new order could rise. One not built on the whims of kings or the dictates of unseen gods, but on something more absolute—karma. It was not divine decree that would decide the future, nor the privilege of birthright. Only actions. Only the weight of one's own deeds.

The fire at the center of the sages flickered, illuminating seven faces—seven minds shaped by trial, conflict, and revelation.

Tonight, they would forge the laws that would define Karma Yug.

Rudrayan, The Hammer of Justice, stepped forward. *"The world has collapsed under the weight of greed, blind power, and cruelty. If we do not shape its laws now, it will fall into worse ruin. Karma must be the law—but what does that mean?"*

The sages turned to one another, their expressions etched with the weight of the world yet to be rebuilt. Each carried a different vision—some shaped by fire and conflict, others by wisdom and restraint. But all knew one thing: the laws they forged tonight would be the foundation upon which Karma Yug would stand, or the cracks through which it would fall. Each would fight not for themselves, but for the truth they believed the world needed most.

The First Law: No Birthright, Only Deed

"No man shall inherit power, wealth, or privilege through bloodline. Only karma shall dictate one's standing in the world."

Rudrayan's Perspective – Justice Must Be Earned, Not Inherited

Rudrayan's voice was unyielding, each word striking like a hammer upon an anvil. *"Power is not a birthright. A fool born into wealth remains a fool, no matter how fine the silk he wears. A tyrant's son is not born to rule; he is born to forge his own fate, just like every other soul. To inherit power without proving one's worth is to invite decay into the foundations of society. A throne unearned is a throne doomed to corruption. This cycle shall end here, forever."*

A noble, his robe tattered but his pride unbroken, scoffed. His once-gilded hands clenched into fists, his voice thick with defiance. *"Without rulers, there will be only chaos! Without legacy, there is no order! If men are left to rise and fall without lineage to guide them, what stops an unworthy fool from seizing power? Will a child born in rags be fit to rule over men? Will a kingdom built by generations be left in the hands of chance? You call this justice? I call it ruin!"*

Anirvan's Perspective – Strength Must Be Proven, Not Assumed

Anirvan, The Flame of Courage, stood firm, his stance unwavering like a mountain before a storm. *"Then let men rise by their actions, not by the accidents of their birth. A leader must prove himself in the crucible of life—through trial, through struggle, through the fire of his own karma. If he stumbles, let him rise again. If he fails, let him learn. But let no man sit upon a throne he has not earned with his own blood, sweat, and sacrifice."*

The noble's fists clenched, his voice edged with desperation and defiance. *"And if my son is worthy? If he has trained in battle, studied wisdom, and proven himself stronger than any other? Will you still deny him his rightful place? Should a father's efforts mean nothing, his legacy cast aside, simply because he was born to me?"*

Satyavrat's Perspective – Truth Over Tradition

Satyavrat, The Bearer of Truth, stepped forward, his piercing gaze locking onto the noble. *"Then let him prove it—not through lineage, but through action. If he is truly worthy, let his deeds speak louder than his name. A title handed down is an empty shell, but a title earned is unshakable. A kingdom ruled by the unworthy is no kingdom at all—it is a prison built upon deception, waiting to collapse under the weight of its own lies. Let karma, not bloodlines, determine the rulers of Karma Yug."*

Vidyatman's Perspective – Knowledge Must Not Be Hoarded

Vidyatman, The Keeper of Knowledge, spoke next, his voice measured and deliberate. *"Wealth of the mind is the only inheritance that should be passed, for true power lies not in gold or thrones, but in wisdom and understanding. If a scholar's son is wise, he shall become a scholar—not because of his lineage, but because he has learned and proven his worth. If a warrior's daughter is strong, she shall wield a sword—not because her father fought before her, but because she has honed her strength. Titles, like knowledge, must not be given—they must be earned. To hand them down without merit is to reduce them to hollow symbols, devoid of meaning. Karma Yug will be a world where each individual stands on the foundation of their own learning and actions, not on the shadows of their ancestors."*

Yuktashakti's Perspective – Fate Belongs to the Individual

Yuktashakti, The Weaver of Fate, answered, her voice carrying the weight of unseen threads, the echoes of past lives and futures yet unwritten. *"If a man's fate is decided at birth, then why does he live? What purpose does he serve beyond fulfilling a script he never wrote? Karma Yug will not allow fate to be dictated by the past. Every soul shall weave its own path, stitch by stitch, action by action. The threads of destiny are not shackles—they are choices waiting to be made. In this new world, no name shall grant power, and no lineage shall dictate worth. Only through their own hands will men and women shape what they become."*

Nirvansh's Perspective – Desire Must Be Controlled

Nirvansh, The Master of Desire, stepped forward last, his voice calm but carrying the weight of a truth often ignored. *"Greed hides behind inheritance. 'I deserve this,' men say, though they have done nothing to earn it. A son born in a palace believes himself fit to rule, not because of wisdom or strength, but because of walls built by another's hands. In Karma Yug, such illusions shall not persist. Let men desire, but let their desires be worthy. Let them crave knowledge, not blind power; mastery, not idleness; virtue, not vanity. Desire itself is not the enemy—it is unchecked, unearned desire that poisons the soul. Let men chase greatness, but let them build it themselves, brick by brick, act by act."*

Karunesh's Perspective – A Just Society Must Protect the Weak

Karunesh, The Vessel of Mercy, spoke last, his tone gentler but no less resolute. *"But we must not cast the children of the fallen into suffering. A king's son shall not inherit a throne, but neither shall he be left to wander aimlessly in the shadows of his father's downfall. A child should not bear the weight of a past he did not create, nor should he be granted privileges he did not earn. Let every child have the same chance to rise—not as beggars, forced to scrape for survival, but as seekers of karma, given the tools to forge their own destinies. A just world does not shun the innocent; it lifts them so they may walk their own path."*

And so, the **First Law** was set:

No birthright, only deed. A soul rises not by lineage, but by karma.

It was a proclamation that shattered centuries of tradition. The assembled crowd murmured, torn between awe and apprehension. Some nobles clenched their fists, their entire existence built upon inheritance now reduced to irrelevance. Warriors who had spent their lives defending a lineage now faced a world where their loyalty would belong to merit, not names.

A farmer in the crowd whispered, *"Then my son has the same right to rise as the son of a king?"*

Satyavrat answered, his voice steady, *"Your son has only what he earns. No less, no more."*

A young scholar, still clutching the scrolls of a forgotten kingdom, stepped forward. *"But will the wise still guide? Or do we cast away knowledge as we cast away bloodlines?"*

Vidyatman nodded. *"Wisdom is not lost. It is no longer hoarded. In Karma Yug, the learned shall teach, the strong shall protect, the just shall lead—but none shall be placed above another by the accident of birth."*

A silence settled over the land. This law would not be easy to accept. But it would be just. And in time, it would reshape the world.

The Second Law: The Measure of Justice

"Justice shall be measured not by the act alone, but by the intent behind it. Punishment shall reflect the karma, not the crime."

Rudrayan's Perspective – Justice Must Not Be Blind

Rudrayan's voice was sharp, his eyes scanning the crowd with the weight of one who had seen the failures of justice firsthand. *"Justice in Kalyug was a hammer that struck blindly, crushing both the wicked and the desperate alike. It made no distinction between those who stole out of greed and those who stole out of hunger. It called both the oppressor and the oppressed criminals, without ever pausing to ask why. Justice, without wisdom, is not justice at all—it is cruelty wrapped in law. This shall end. In Karma Yug, punishment will not be a sword that falls upon all without question, but a scale that weighs both action and intent, ensuring that no man is condemned without understanding the burden of his karma."*

A farmer stepped forward, his ribs showing beneath his torn tunic, his voice heavy with desperation and uncertainty. *"If I steal to feed my starving child, am I the same as a rich man who steals for greed? When my hands tremble as I take a loaf of bread, knowing it is my only chance to keep my child alive, do I bear the same karma as one who hoards wealth while others suffer? If the law punishes only the act, does it not ignore the suffering that led to it?"*

Satyavrat's Perspective – Truth in Judgment

Satyavrat's expression remained calm, yet his voice carried the weight of unshakable truth. *"No. A starving man does not steal—he survives. His act is not one of greed, but of desperation, driven by a world that has denied him the means to live. Survival cannot be judged as greed, for the law must recognize the difference between necessity and indulgence. Justice must not punish hunger; it must understand the suffering that leads to it. But even survival, though justifiable, does not erase consequence. Let there be a path where he can restore what was taken, not through punishment, but through purpose—through labor, through service, through redemption."*

Karunesh's Perspective – Mercy Within Justice

Karunesh placed a hand on the man's shoulder, his eyes filled with understanding yet firm resolve. *"But balance must be restored. If you take, you must give back—not as punishment, but as redemption. Taking something, even out of desperation, leaves an imbalance in the world. It is not justice to punish a man for hunger, but neither is it just to allow imbalance to grow unchecked. Let your actions bring balance once more. If you have taken food, let your hands labor to provide food for others. If you have taken shelter, let your strength build shelter for another. Redemption is not suffering—it is the act of restoring harmony."*

Anirvan's Perspective – Strength Without Tyranny

Anirvan's voice was unwavering, yet laced with a fire that demanded accountability. *"But what of those who kill? Who destroy? Not out of desperation, not out of protection, but for power, for greed, for pleasure? A man who steals out of hunger may yet redeem himself, but a man who takes a life without remorse—what redemption is there for him? Can a man who kills for his own gain ever truly undo his karma? Or is his fate sealed the moment his blade tastes innocent blood?"*

Vidyatman's Perspective – Knowledge as Judgment

Vidyatman answered, his voice carrying the wisdom of ages. *"Then let their karma shape their fate. But let no man be punished in ignorance. Justice in Karma Yug shall not be a weapon wielded by the powerful against the weak, nor a blind force that strikes without understanding. Every action stems from intent, and knowledge must guide judgment. A man who does wrong without knowing its weight is not beyond redemption; he must first be taught, made to understand the consequences of his actions. But once he knows, and still chooses the path of darkness, then karma shall deal with him without mercy. Justice must be understanding, but it must never be weak."*

Yuktashakti's Perspective – Justice Must Evolve

Yuktashakti added, her voice carrying the quiet certainty of one who understood the delicate weave of fate. *"And no man shall be bound forever by his past. If he seeks redemption, it shall be allowed, but only through his actions, not merely his regret. Karma does not shackle—it teaches, it corrects, and it offers a path forward. A man who once walked in darkness must prove his commitment to light. He must not only seek forgiveness but create balance through deeds that outweigh his past transgressions. Karma is not a cage—it is a path, but one that must be walked with intention and resolve."*

Nirvansh's Perspective – Unchecked Desires Lead to Chaos

Nirvansh, his voice deep and resonant, spoke last, his words carrying the weight of timeless wisdom. *"But let no man think that desire is an excuse. Desire, when unrestrained, is the root of destruction. A man who kills for power shall not wield it for long—karma will strip him of his dominion, and he will know the emptiness of his ambition. If a man destroys for pleasure, let him taste ruin, for his joy is built on suffering. Justice is not merely a force of consequence; it is a force of transformation. It shall be both weight and wind—an anchor for those who learn and rise, and a storm that sweeps away those who refuse to change. Let every soul be given the chance to master their desires, but let none escape the fate they forge with their own hands."*

And so, the **Second Law** was set:

Justice shall be measured, not blind.

The declaration sent ripples through the gathered crowd. Some nodded in solemn understanding, while others exchanged wary glances. For generations, justice had been an iron blade—unyielding, indiscriminate. Now, it would become something far more complex, far more deliberate.

A former soldier, his body lined with old scars, stepped forward. *"Then who decides intent? Who holds the scales? If justice is no longer blind, does it not risk being swayed by emotion?"*

Rudrayan answered, his tone unshaken. *"Justice is not blind—it sees clearly, but without prejudice. Those who judge will not rule from arrogance or personal bias, but with the wisdom of karma. The weight of an action will be examined in full, not merely the surface of a crime."*

A merchant, whose wealth had once shielded him from consequence, clenched his jaw. *"And what if a man with wealth seeks mercy, weaving lies of necessity? What stops him from escaping judgment while the weak still suffer?"*

Satyavrat met his gaze steadily. *"Karma does not bow to gold. A man's deception may fool others, but it will not fool the weight of his own actions. No bribe can lighten a burden that grows heavier with every dishonest act."*

A mother, clutching the hand of her child, hesitated before speaking. *"And if a man seeks redemption? If he wishes to right his wrongs, will his past always define him?"*

Yuktashakti's voice was calm. *"A man is not shackled to his past, but neither can he walk away from it without effort. Let him prove through action that he is more than the sum of his misdeeds. Redemption is not given—it is earned."*

The murmurs among the crowd shifted, some voices filled with hope, others with unease. Justice had been rewritten, no longer an unfeeling force but a balance of action and consequence.

And in time, the world would learn to wield it.

The Third Law: The Right to Choose

"Every man and woman shall be free to choose their own path, but no choice shall come without consequence."

The sages stood in silence, watching the crowd before them. The weight of justice had been laid, but now came the question of **free will**—the foundation upon which Karma Yug would stand. Should men be allowed to forge their own destinies, unshackled by fate? Or should the sages set a path for them, ensuring that chaos did not return?

Rudrayan's Perspective – Choice is Power, and Power Must Be Earned

Rudrayan's voice was steady and firm. *"In Kalyug, men blamed the gods, their rulers, and fate itself for their misery. 'I had no choice,' they cried. 'I was forced into suffering.' But in Karma Yug, no man shall claim he was bound. Every soul shall be free to shape their own path, but let them also bear the burden of the choices they make. Power without accountability leads to ruin, and we will not allow that ruin to return."*

A young warrior, his face scarred from past battles, stepped forward. *"And what of those who are misguided? What if a man chooses poorly—not out of malice, but ignorance?"*

Vidyatman's Perspective – Knowledge Must Guide Choice

Vidyatman, The Keeper of Knowledge, nodded. *"No choice should be made in ignorance. A man who walks blindly into fire is no freer than one who is pushed. If men are to choose, let them be given wisdom. Let them understand the weight of their actions before they take them. Let there be no excuses of ignorance in Karma Yug."*

Nirvansh's Perspective – Desire and Choice Are One

Nirvansh, his voice deep and unwavering, spoke next. *"In Kalyug, men let their desires rule them, claiming that temptation was too strong to resist. They surrendered to greed, lust, and wrath, saying, 'I could not help it.' That, too, ends now. A man is not a slave to his desires. If he chooses indulgence over restraint, let him bear the consequences. If he chooses wisdom over recklessness, let him reap the rewards. Let men understand that their choices are their own, and their karma will follow them."*

Karunesh's Perspective – Freedom Must Not Lead to Harm

A mother clutched her child tightly and asked, *"And what if a man's choice harms another? Will he still be free?"*

Karunesh, The Vessel of Mercy, answered gently, *"Freedom does not grant the right to harm. If a man's choice brings suffering to another, then his karma will correct him. No freedom shall be so absolute that it tramples upon the freedom of another. Let men choose, but let them understand that their choices will not be without cost."*

Anirvan's Perspective – Strength of Will in Action

A warrior raised his sword, his expression questioning. *"And what of war? What if I choose battle? If I take up arms, will I be punished?"*

Anirvan's eyes burned like embers. *"Then you will bear war's judgment. If you choose battle for greed, you shall find yourself consumed by it. If you fight for justice, you shall be carried forward by karma. No sword is evil. It is the hand that wields it that shapes its fate. Choose war, and you shall bear its weight. Choose peace, and you must defend it with equal strength."*

Yuktashakti's Perspective – Fate is Woven by Choice

Yuktashakti stepped forward, her voice filled with quiet certainty. *"Choice is not merely an action—it is the very thread of karma. Every decision we make, no matter how small, weaves the fabric of our destiny. If men are free to choose, then they must also accept that their fate is their own creation. No more shall they curse the heavens for their misfortune, for their hands shall be the ones that shape it."*

Satyavrat's Perspective – Truth in Freedom

The final words came from Satyavrat, his gaze piercing through the uncertainty. *"In Karma Yug, there will be no kings to command men, no gods to decide for them. Let every soul stand accountable for their own path. Let there be no deception, no false comforts. The truth is simple—your choices are yours alone, and karma will answer to them."*

And so, the **Third Law** was set:

Every choice is free, but every choice has a price.

The crowd murmured, some fearful, some determined. Freedom was both a gift and a trial. The sages had declared it so—no longer would men hide behind fate, rulers, or gods.

The burden of destiny now belonged to them alone. And so, beneath the vast heavens and upon the scarred earth, a new age was born—not through the will of gods nor the decree of rulers, but through the choices of men. The Seven Sages had spoken, but the true test lay ahead. Would the people rise to the challenge, embracing the weight of their own karma? Or would they falter, yearning for the chains they had so long been bound by? Only time, and their deeds, would tell.

Balancing the Scales

The sages sat in a semicircle within the great cavern of creation, their forms illuminated by the flickering golden torches along the stone walls. The air was thick with tension. The echoes of their voices clashed like waves in a stormy ocean, for the fate of Karma Yug rested upon their deliberations.

Rudrayan, his arms folded across his broad chest, spoke first. His voice was firm, unwavering.

"Karma is absolute. If we are to build a just world, we cannot afford leniency. Every action must bear a consequence, or we risk falling into the chaos of Kalyug again. The thief who steals must be punished, no matter the reason. If we make exceptions, we invite disorder."

Satyavrat nodded in agreement. *"Truth must not bend to circumstance. If a starving man steals, his hunger is unfortunate but does not change the nature of his deed. To steal is to commit a crime, and justice must be impartial."*

Karunesh's eyes darkened with sorrow as he stepped forward, his voice carrying the weight of compassion. *"And yet, must we not consider the intent behind an action? A man who steals because his child is dying of hunger is not the same as a king who hoards food while his people starve. Where is the justice in punishing them equally? We are not here to create a world of rigid laws but of true balance!"*

A low murmur rippled through the sages. Nirvansh, the master of desire, rubbed his chin thoughtfully. *"But if we begin down the path of interpretation, where do we draw the line? What if a warrior slaughters hundreds in battle but claims it was for protection? What if a liar deceives but says it was to avoid harm? If karma is twisted by justification, it loses its essence."*

Anirvan, the flame of courage, leaned forward, his eyes blazing. *"Then let each soul face its own trial! Let the punishment be proportionate, not merely equal. If a starving man steals, let him repay his debt by feeding another. If a tyrant withholds grain, let him live among the hungry and know their suffering!"*

Vidyatman, the keeper of knowledge, stroked his long white beard, his voice calm but piercing. *"Balance is not found in extremes. If we enforce rigid justice, we will create fear, not righteousness. But if we grant too much mercy, we may enable corruption. We must construct a system that understands both the deed and the doer. The weight of a crime is not in the act alone but in the intent that shaped it."*

Yuktashakti, the weaver of fate, who had remained silent until now, finally spoke, her voice like the whisper of the cosmos. *"We do not stand at the end of a cycle but at its dawn. What we set in motion today will define Karma Yug for eternity. Justice must be tempered with wisdom. If we fail to create the right balance, we will doom this age before it even begins."*

The argument swelled again, voices rising and falling.

Rudrayan clenched his fists. *"A world without strict karmic justice is a world where the wicked thrive. I will not be part of a creation where sin is excused!"*

Karunesh shook his head. *"And I will not be part of a creation where kindness is discarded as weakness!"*

Anirvan interjected, *"Then let us define the cases where justice will be absolute! Crimes rooted in greed, cruelty, and power-lust must bear the harshest consequences. A ruler who betrays his people for his own gain shall be stripped of his power and made to serve as the lowest among them. A murderer who kills for pleasure shall wander the land as a lost soul, unable to find peace until he redeems every life he took."*

Satyavrat added, *"But those who commit crimes from desperation or ignorance must be given paths to redemption. The thief who steals bread to survive shall work in the fields to cultivate more food, not rot in chains. A liar who deceives to protect another shall bear the burden of honesty until he restores trust."*

Yuktashakti closed her eyes and whispered, *"Then the laws of Karma Yug will be built on duality—some sins will demand strict retribution, while others will allow atonement. Fate will not be blind, but neither will it be merciless."*

The cavern trembled as their emotions flared. The torches flickered wildly, as though the very universe held its breath, waiting for the verdict of the sages.

Then, suddenly, an ancient voice echoed through the chamber. Deep and resonant, it silenced all debate. The air itself seemed to tremble, and the flickering torches steadied as if held in the grip of an unseen force. The voice carried the weight of creation, of time itself bending to listen.

It was Brahma.

"Enough," the Creator's voice thundered. "You are not here to fight like mortals. You are here to forge the laws of a new world. Justice must not be blind to suffering, nor must mercy shield evil. Find your path, or this age will crumble before it even stands."

The sages fell silent, their eyes meeting in reluctant understanding. Vishnu stepped forward, his celestial presence radiating calm. *"There will come times when one must choose between the absolute truth and what is right for the greater good. Dharma is not always black and white, and in those moments, the burden of choice will rest on the karma of the doer."*

Shiva's voice, deep and resolute, followed. *"Karma is the path you carve, the consequence you bear. Choose wisely, for the laws we set today will not decide fate—actions will. And in the end, Karma Yug will not judge you. It will merely reflect what you have chosen to become."* The debate was far from over, but one thing was certain: the world they would build would not be simple. The battle between justice and mercy was not one to be settled in words alone—it would be tested in the souls of every being to come.

And the true weight of karma would soon be revealed.

First Test of the New Order

The village of Svarnapur lay in the shadow of a crumbling past. Once a thriving hub in the late Kalyug era, it had been ruled by a cruel leader, Dandhiraj. Known for his ruthless governance, he had extracted heavy tributes, enslaved weaker villagers, and crushed dissent without mercy. Under his rule, justice had meant servitude, and the weak had no voice.

But Kalyug had ended.

Now, in the uncertain dawn of Karma Yug, Dandhiraj stood before the Seven Sages, his once-imposing figure reduced to that of a humbled man. The people of Svarnapur had dragged him to their assembly, voices rising in fury.

"He burned our fields when we couldn't pay his taxes!"

"My father died in his dungeons!"

"He laughed when our children starved!"

The cries of the villagers formed a storm around the sages. Dandhiraj knelt, his hands folded, his forehead pressed to the cold earth.

"I have changed," he murmured. "The gods have taken away my power, my wealth, and my illusions. I see the weight of my sins now. Give me a chance to atone."

The first test had arrived.

The Debate of the Sages

The Seven Sages looked at one another, their minds and principles clashing.

Rudrayan, the Hammer of Justice, stepped forward first. *"His past karma is clear. He ruled with cruelty and greed, and the suffering he caused cannot be erased with mere words. In*

Karma Yug, the past still holds power over one's destiny. He must face justice."

Karunesh, the Vessel of Mercy, placed a hand on Rudrayan's arm. *"But if Karma Yug is to be different from Kalyug, we must allow redemption. If a man seeks to change, should we not let him?"*

Satyavrat, the Bearer of Truth, closed his eyes. *"The truth is that men can lie. A man can feign change only to seize power again. We must test him."*

Anirvan, the Flame of Courage, turned to the villagers. *"If we allow him to live among you, will you ever trust him again?"*

A woman stepped forward. *"He made my husband disappear,"* she whispered. *"If he lives, I will always fear him."*

Vidyatman, the Keeper of Knowledge, stroked his beard. *"Perhaps our decision should not be made in haste. The mind can change, but habits are hard to break. What proof do we have that he is truly different?"*

Yuktashakti, the Weaver of Fate, looked at Dandhiraj. *"If he seeks redemption, let fate decide. We shall give him a trial, a test where he must prove his change—not to us, but to those he harmed."*

Nirvansh, the Master of Desire, nodded. *"If he seeks atonement, then he must serve. Stripping him of power is not enough. Let him rebuild what he destroyed."*

The Trial of Redemption

After much debate, the sages decreed a trial. Dandhiraj would be given a chance—not through empty words, but through action. He would be assigned to the harshest labor: rebuilding homes, tending to fields, and serving those he had wronged without authority or privilege. His every action would be watched, and his redemption would not be determined by himself, but by the people he once oppressed.

"If you have truly changed," Rudrayan declared, "then let the ones you harmed be your judges."

Dandhiraj bowed. *"I accept."*

For months, he toiled, plowing fields, carrying bricks, and healing what he once destroyed. At first, the villagers scoffed, refusing to believe in his transformation. But time revealed the truth. When a plague struck Svarnapur, he was the first to tend to the sick. When the rains threatened the harvest, he shielded crops with his own hands. Slowly, resentment softened into reluctant acceptance.

One day, the woman whose husband had vanished approached him. *"You took everything from me,"* she said. *"But I see that you grieve your past now."*

But Dandhiraj was not the only one facing judgment.

The Case of Raghunandan

As the village deliberated over Dandhiraj, another man, Raghunandan, was brought before the sages. His story was whispered with horror—during Kalyug, in his hunger for land and power, he had slain his own father and two brothers, forging documents to seize their wealth. His crime had been buried under the corruption of the era, but now, in Karma Yug, there was no place for such darkness to hide.

"I was blinded by greed," Raghunandan admitted. "But when the world crumbled, I lost everything. My children left me, my wealth turned to dust, and guilt burned me from within. I have spent years atoning, feeding orphans, giving away the very land I stole. I beg for a chance to truly serve."

The sages were silent. Unlike Dandhiraj, whose sins were political, Raghunandan had committed the ultimate betrayal—shedding his own family's blood. Could such a man ever be redeemed?

Rudrayan's voice was firm. *"Murder cannot be undone. Your victims cry for justice."*

Karunesh hesitated. *"Yet he has already punished himself. His suffering is immense."*

Satyavrat raised his hand. *"If truth is our guide, then his past must not be ignored. But if Karma Yug is to be just, his fate should not be ours to decide alone."*

The villagers spoke among themselves. Some argued that no atonement could erase the crime of fratricide. Others saw a broken man, haunted and repentant.

Finally, Yuktashakti spoke. *"Let him spend the rest of his days serving the children he orphaned—the young and abandoned. Let him build, not destroy. Only they shall judge whether he has redeemed himself."*

Raghunandan wept. *"I accept."*

The Struggle for Freedom

In the bustling heart of Svarnapur, Sumedha's footsteps echoed softly on the dust-covered road as she approached the assembly of sages. Her attire was fine, the finest of silks in the village, a stark contrast to the humbler clothes worn by most. Her father, a wealthy Brahmin, had raised her with high expectations, binding her future to the customs of their family and community.

"I wish to marry Raghav," she said, standing tall before the assembly of sages, her voice clear but filled with quiet defiance. *"But he is of a lower caste. My family and community would never accept it."*

The sages exchanged glances. They had witnessed the transformation of the village, the dissolution of old ways, yet they knew that deeply entrenched beliefs would not change easily.

Sumedha's eyes sparkled with a mixture of hope and pain. *"Raghav is a man of integrity, of heart. He has proved himself in the work he has done for the community. Why should the accident of birth stand in the way of our happiness?"*

The murmurs of the villagers grew louder, some supportive, others disapproving. But it was clear that the tension between tradition and personal freedom had reached a boiling point.

Rudrayan, the Hammer of Justice, stepped forward with a stern gaze. *"Tradition has served to protect the community in the past. The rules exist to maintain order. Should we break them now for the whims of a few?"*

Rudrayan's words reflected the old world where justice and order were tied to the structure of society. His role as the enforcer of justice was clear, and he felt that a marriage between different castes might jeopardize the new order, undermining the social balance they were trying to build in Karma Yug.

But **Vidyatman, the Keeper of Knowledge**, gently countered, his voice thoughtful yet firm. *"Is not the pursuit of knowledge, the very essence of Karma Yug, to allow growth and transformation? We are not simply passing down the old ways, but seeking wisdom in new ways. Should we not question the shackles of tradition if they bind our hearts?"*

Vidyatman's influence steered the discussion toward enlightenment, suggesting that wisdom and knowledge from the past should not be blindly followed, especially if it prevented personal growth and freedom.

Yuktashakti, the Weaver of Fate, then spoke, her tone soft but powerful. *"The fabric of fate has been altered with the advent of Karma Yug. Freedom is the thread that will weave the future. If the heart chooses truth, and if destiny is not tied to caste, then who are we to deny the choice of these two souls?"*

Her words were like a gentle wind, encouraging others to see that fate, as it had been understood, was no longer absolute. The force of destiny could no longer be dictated by birth or past ties. The villagers, many of whom had experienced oppression based on their own birth status, felt her words resonate deeply.

But Sumedha's father, unwilling to lose his grip on the world he knew, was still adamant. *"You speak of fate, but what of society? What of the reputation of our family, of our village? Will we allow the foundations of our world to crumble?"*

This time, **Satyavrat, the Bearer of Truth**, stepped forward, his eyes sharp and piercing. *"If truth is our guide, then we must not deceive ourselves into believing that the world must remain as it was. The truth is that love, loyalty, and choice cannot be confined by ancient laws. Sumedha's choice to marry Raghav is not a betrayal of tradition; it is a declaration of her truth."*

Satyavrat's words were a direct challenge to the foundations that Sumedha's father clung to. He reminded everyone that truth, no matter how uncomfortable, was the guiding principle of Karma Yug. If Sumedha's love was real and her intentions pure, then that was the truth they should honor.

Sumedha's father, hearing these words, clenched his fists. For the first time, doubt crept into his heart. Could he truly force his daughter into a life she did not choose? The inner conflict began to surface in him, but he was not ready to relent.

Karunesh, the Vessel of Mercy, then placed a hand gently on Sumedha's shoulder. *"Mercy begins with understanding. You have been a product of this world's traditions, but that does not mean you cannot break free. The heart that loves should be allowed to flourish, for that is the true source of kindness."*

Karunesh's compassion for Sumedha softened the hearts of many. His words pointed to the power of love and mercy, emphasizing that mercy wasn't just about pardoning sins, but about allowing personal freedom to thrive and evolve.

Finally, **Nirvansh, the Master of Desire**, spoke, his voice calm yet profound. *"Desire is not the enemy of virtue— it is the driver of transformation. If Sumedha desires Raghav, and her love is pure, then this desire has the potential to build a new world, one free from the chains of old systems. Let this union be a symbol of the new order."*

Nirvansh's perspective on desire brought a new light to the discussion. His teachings emphasized that desires, when rooted in purity and intention, could be forces for change rather than corruption. His endorsement of the union gave the sages a clear path forward—they had to allow freedom of choice, even if it meant breaking away from the constraints of tradition.

After a long silence, Rudrayan finally spoke again, his voice softer than before. *"Perhaps I have been too rigid. Freedom, truth, and mercy must guide us in Karma Yug. If the heart is true, and the people support this union, then we must stand with them."*

The villagers were once again called to gather, and as Sumedha and Raghav stood together, the assembly slowly voted on their future. The atmosphere was heavy, the village split. But in the end, it was the voices of those who had been held down by centuries of inequality who spoke the loudest. They supported the union, for they saw in it the promise of a new world—one where birth no longer dictated destiny.

In the end, Sumedha's freedom to choose, and the villagers' acceptance of it, became a symbol of the new age—the dawn of a world where karma, not caste, guided the way.

The Verdict of the Village

As the sun began to set over Svarnapur, the villagers gathered once again in the central square. The air was heavy with anticipation, charged with a blend of uncertainty and hope. The events of the last few days had shaken the very foundations of their beliefs, and now they stood at the crossroads of change, facing the ultimate test of Karma Yug.

The crowd murmured, eyes shifting between Dandhiraj, the once-feared outcast, and Raghunandan, the young man who had dared to challenge the age-old rules of caste. Their fates were now intertwined with that of Sumedha, the girl who had defied tradition by choosing love over societal expectation. The very fabric of their world seemed to be teetering on the brink of something profound, something unknown.

The village that had once stood united against Dandhiraj, seeing him as a threat to their way of life, now looked at him with a new lens. The fear that had once clouded their judgment was fading, replaced by curiosity and, for some, a glimmer of understanding. Dandhiraj had stood before the sages, had undergone trials, and had proven that he was not the villain they had once believed him to be. His actions, though controversial, had led to an awakening in the hearts of many. His transformation, from a pariah to a symbol of Karma Yug's promise, was a testament to the power of change. In a world where karma was now the deciding factor, even those who had once been cast out could find redemption.

Meanwhile, Raghunandan's situation was equally scrutinized, but with a different lens. His love for Sumedha had led him to challenge the unspoken rules of caste, an act that many had viewed as an affront to centuries-old traditions. Yet, in the heart of Karma Yug, it was not the birthright that mattered, but the purity of one's actions and the truth of one's intentions. Sumedha's father, the village patriarch, had been adamant that his daughter's marriage would uphold the integrity of their family name, but his view began to soften as the discussion unfolded. He had been forced to confront his own fears and prejudices, realizing that his daughter's happiness was more important than the weight of societal expectations.

The village stood divided. Half of them could not shake off the old ways, clinging to the comfort of tradition and the stability it promised. They argued that society had functioned for generations under these laws, and to break them would be to risk chaos. The other half, the ones who had witnessed the sages' teachings and the profound changes they were advocating, stood firmly in support of Sumedha and Raghav's union. They believed that Karma Yug was not about adhering to the old ways but about creating a new world where individual freedom, love, and equality could thrive.

As the murmurs died down, **Rudrayan**, the Hammer of Justice, stood tall and addressed the crowd. His voice was strong, yet there was a softness to it now, a newfound understanding. *"We have always believed that justice is about punishment, about enforcing the laws of our ancestors. But the truth that Karma Yug has taught us is that justice must also be about transformation, about redemption. Dandhiraj, once a symbol of everything we feared, has proven that the past does not define the future. His actions, though controversial, have led him here today, and he stands before us as a reminder that even the most broken souls can find a new path."*

There was a long silence as the villagers absorbed Rudrayan's words. The idea that justice was not merely about punishment, but about creating the space for transformation, was a radical departure from everything they had known. It was a concept that, though difficult for many to accept, was slowly beginning to take root in their hearts.

Next, **Satyavrat**, the Bearer of Truth, spoke. His words cut through the tension like a knife, bringing clarity to the murky waters of doubt. *"Truth is not a rigid construct, bound by the chains of tradition. It is fluid, it is alive, and it grows with us. Sumedha's truth is her love for Raghav, and that truth must be honored. We must ask ourselves: who are we to deny the truth of the heart? In this new era, we cannot allow the past to dictate who we are or who we can become."*

His words echoed in the air, resonating deeply with those who had been uncertain. In the presence of the sages, the villagers began to see that Karma Yug was not merely about maintaining the status quo—it was about breaking free from the constraints of the past to create a more just and equitable world.

Vidyatman, the Keeper of Knowledge, added his voice to the mix. *"We are in the age of knowledge, where learning is not bound by the scriptures alone but by experience and reason. The knowledge we seek is not just in the words of our ancestors but in the hearts of those who are brave enough to follow their own path. Sumedha's choice to marry Raghav is an act of wisdom, not folly. It is an expression of the knowledge that we are all capable of growth, of changing the very fabric of our society."*

As the sages spoke, the villagers began to feel the shift in the air. The old way of thinking, where caste determined everything, was slowly unraveling. The very heart of

Karma Yug was taking shape before their eyes—a world where karma, not caste, would determine one's destiny.

Finally, **Karunesh,** the Vessel of Mercy, spoke with a compassion that moved even the hardest of hearts. *"Mercy is not just about forgiveness—it is about understanding, about allowing room for others to grow, to evolve. If we cannot show mercy to those who love freely, who seek to build their own lives, then what kind of society are we creating? A society that binds the heart and soul in chains of old beliefs? No. We must show mercy, for it is mercy that will allow us all to move forward together."*

With the words of the sages guiding them, the village stood at a crossroads, but one where the light of Karma Yug was beginning to shine through. The final decision was made not by force or fear, but by the collective will of the people. The marriage between Sumedha and Raghav would be allowed, and in that moment, the old walls that separated them from each other—walls built by caste and tradition—began to crumble.

The First Lesson of Karma Yug

In the end, the judgment that was passed on Dandhiraj, Raghunandan, and Sumedha became more than just an individual decision—it became a statement for the future. The first test of Karma Yug had reached its conclusion, and with it, the first great lesson of the new era was learned: **justice and mercy must walk hand in hand. Karma was not simply about punishment, but about transformation. It was not merely about adhering to** tradition, but about allowing freedom—the freedom to choose, to love, to change.

The villagers had seen that to be truly just was to recognize the humanity in others, to understand that sometimes the path of the heart needed to be honored even when it defied convention. They had learned that Karma Yug was not a time to punish those who dared to challenge the old ways, but a time to embrace change, to let go of the past, and to allow a new world to rise—one built on the foundation of individual freedom, love, and the power of transformation.

And so, as the verdict was passed, the village of Svarnapur stood not as it had before—bound by old customs—but as a beacon of the new world, a world where Karma Yug would continue to shape the future, one choice at a time.

The Divide of Karma: Voices of Dissent

Raghav: *"Karma! Karma! Karma!"* he shouted, his face flushed with frustration. *"What is this madness?!"* His hands trembled as he slammed his hammer onto the anvil. *"How can we trust this? How can we live like this?! Where are the rules? Where's the certainty?!"*

Kavita: *"Rules? Certainty?"* she snapped, her voice sharp, *"Did the old ways bring us peace? Did the old laws save us from suffering? No! We were crushed under the weight of those so-called rules. Karma is the answer, Raghav! It's about what we do, not what we're told to do!"* Her fists clenched, her eyes burning with anger.

Raghav: *"You think this is better? You think karma will save us when we don't even know what's right or wrong anymore?!"* He swung his arms wide, his voice growing louder. *"The world is chaos! And you want to put our lives in the hands of an invisible force?!"*

Kavita: *"At least it's not the hands of tyrants!"* she shot back, her voice thick with bitterness. *"The old gods, the kings, they destroyed everything. Look around us! We have nothing left! But Karma Yug—this new world—at least it gives us the chance to rebuild. It gives us hope!"*

Dinesh: *"Hope?"* Dinesh's voice was low, dangerous, as he stepped forward, his eyes cold. *"This is madness! You all are deluding yourselves! Without rules, without laws, this place will fall into anarchy. Don't you see it? If everyone just does whatever they want, society will tear itself apart!"*

Raghav: *"Yes! That's exactly what I'm saying!"* Raghav pointed at Dinesh, his voice shaking with the intensity of his emotions. *"We need discipline, we need order! Without it, there's no foundation! Without laws, without punishment, what is stopping anyone from turning this world into a wild beast's den?!"*

Kavita: *"You're blinded by fear, Raghav! You always were!"* Kavita's voice cracked with frustration, her body tense. *"You can't see that karma is the only thing that can set us free from all this mess. You just want to hold onto the chains of the past, but we can't go back! We have to move forward!"*

Sundar (a villager): *"Hold on!"* Sundar raised his voice, trying to bring some balance. *"What if we do something in between? Something between what we've had and this new way? Maybe we can have rules, but not like before. Maybe it's not about strict punishment but about responsibility for our actions—karma, yes, but with some structure!"*

Raghav: *"See? Even Sundar gets it! You can't just let people do whatever they want. There has to be some guidance! The sages, they don't get it! They think karma is enough, but they don't know what it's like to live in the dirt, to feel hunger, to see families torn apart. They're so far removed from real life, it's laughable!"*

Asha (another villager): *"You're the one who doesn't get it, Raghav!" Asha's voice rose, a sharp edge in it. "You think the old ways worked? They didn't. That's why we're here, living in the ruins of what was once 'order.' We're here because those old laws failed us! The sages are showing us the way to something better, and you want to tear it down because you're too afraid to trust in something you can't see!"*

Dinesh: *"Afraid? Afraid of what?!" Dinesh growled, stepping forward, his chest heaving. "Afraid of chaos? Afraid of what might happen if we don't have control?! Without control, there's no peace! Without control, the world burns! You think karma can stop a beast like that? It will devour us all!"*

Kavita: *"You're wrong, Dinesh!" Kavita's voice trembled, but her words were filled with fire. "We've been devoured already! All we have left is this new chance, this new way. The sages may not have all the answers, but they're the only ones who are trying to guide us out of this madness! The law of Karma Yug is what we need. Not your iron fist!"*

Raghav: *"No!" Raghav slammed his hand onto the ground, his frustration boiling over. "What we need is certainty! We need laws that can be written down, enforced! You can't just live by some abstract idea. What happens when someone's karma goes wrong, huh? Who pays for it then? Who cleans up that mess?"*

Kavita: *"We clean it up!" she yelled, her voice filled with a kind of desperate strength. "We, the people. We are the ones who live by it. We're the ones who shape this world. Karma Yug gives us that responsibility, that power, that freedom!"*

Dinesh: *"Freedom? Freedom is a lie if there's no order to back it up!" Dinesh's words were like a thunderclap, loud and unforgiving. "Without order, freedom is chaos! It will eat us alive! And you know what happens when chaos takes over? It destroys everything!"*

Asha: *"Then what do you want, Dinesh? A return to slavery? A return to the past, where everything was decided for us? Where we had no choice, no voice?" Asha stepped forward, her voice cutting through the air. "You can't control people's hearts with fear anymore. The old ways failed. We can't go back. We have to trust in karma!"*

The Sages' Lament: Watching the World They Created Tear Apart

The conflict seemed to reach its breaking point. Voices clashed like thunder, faces twisted in anger, and the once unified village now stood divided, torn apart by its own people's frustration. The sages, watching from a distant hill, stood frozen in the winds of their own doubt. This was the battle they had warned of—the struggle for the soul of Karma Yug, fought not with swords but with the destructive power of words.

Satyavrat, the Bearer of Truth, his heart heavy, clenched his fists until his nails dug into his palms. His usually unwavering composure faltered as he gazed at the chaos below.

Satyavrat: *"What have we done?"* His voice was a low murmur, almost lost in the wind, but the agony in it was undeniable. *"Is this what the truth brings? This pain, this madness? I have spoken of truth all my life... but how can it be true if it shatters the very foundation of the world we sought to rebuild?"* His eyes were filled with sorrow, as if he were witnessing the destruction of something he had once believed in so firmly.

Yuktashakti, the Weaver of Fate, her brow furrowed, stood beside him, her arms crossed. The wind tugged at her robes, but she didn't feel it. The storm below, the one created by the people's anguish, felt like it had infiltrated her very soul.

Yuktashakti: *"How can we leave them like this, Satyavrat? How can we watch as they fight and destroy themselves in the name of what we tried to give them?"* Her voice trembled with the weight of unshed tears. *"We spoke of mercy, of freedom... but now, I see that all they want is control. All they want is certainty, something solid they can touch, something that doesn't slip through their fingers like sand."*

Satyavrat: *"But we gave them the foundation they needed, Yuktashakti! Karma—self-reliance, responsibility. They must understand that fate is in their own hands, not bound by rigid laws!"* His voice cracked with frustration, his eyes burning with a quiet fire. *"But this... this conflict, this tearing apart of their world—what is the point if they can't see it? Are we destined to watch them burn themselves to the ground? Is this the truth?"* He whispered the last part, his voice breaking with the strain of trying to comprehend what was unfolding before them.

Yuktashakti looked out over the village, her gaze distant but sharp, as if she could see into the hearts of each soul below. She sighed deeply, her voice filled with the weight of the universe.

Yuktashakti: *"Mercy, Satyavrat... Mercy."* The word left her lips like a prayer, an aching plea to the universe for understanding. *"It feels as though they are tearing themselves apart because they cannot understand that mercy does not mean weakness... but strength. They don't see that their anger, their fight for control, is what will destroy them, not save them."*

Satyavrat's eyes softened, and he turned his gaze to the ground beneath their feet. *"I see it now... I see their pain. They are trapped in fear, in uncertainty. We spoke of freedom, but all they hear is the emptiness of it. We spoke of karma, but they cannot grasp its fluidity. How can they? They have been shackled to the old ways for so long, they do not know how to live without the chains."*

Yuktashakti: *"And what of us, Satyavrat? We stand here, powerless, unable to do anything but watch as they drown in their own rage and confusion. We gave them the teachings, but perhaps... perhaps they are not ready for them. Perhaps we were wrong to think that they could understand what we have learned in lifetimes of existence."*

Satyavrat's gaze darkened with the intensity of his inner conflict. *"Did we choose the wrong path for them? Was the truth too much for them to bear? We are sages, Yuktashakti. We were meant to guide them, to teach them. But now... now I fear we have led them to the precipice."*

Yuktashakti: *"I fear it too... But what is left for us to do? To bend and break the laws we have set? To rewrite what Karma Yug truly is? We cannot. We cannot. It is not mercy that will save them, it is their own will, their own desire to change."* She placed a hand over her heart, the burden too much to bear. *"We cannot save them from themselves, Satyavrat. We can only watch, and hope that the seeds of wisdom we planted take root... even if it means watching them struggle first."*

Satyavrat's voice was barely a whisper, filled with the weight of centuries of truth. *"And if they fail, Yuktashakti? If their struggle consumes them?"*

Yuktashakti's voice trembled, but her resolve hardened like steel.

"Then we will mourn, as we must. But we cannot fight their battles for them. We can only hope, pray, and trust that somewhere within them, the teachings will take root. Karma Yug was meant to be a world of choice, of personal responsibility. But it seems we may have forgotten—true change does not come without great pain."

Satyavrat stood there for a long moment, silent, his heart heavy with a sorrow that seemed too much to bear. Then, he looked once more at the chaos below, as if seeking some glimpse of hope in the storm.

Satyavrat: *"May the winds of Karma guide them, for they will need it."*

And so, the sages stood, watching helplessly as the storm of rebellion raged on below. The cries of the villagers echoed through the air, but there was no turning back. Karma Yug was a world built on choice, but the choice, it seemed, was theirs alone to make.

The Sages' Struggle with Power

The ground beneath them cracked and groaned as though the earth itself was torn between two worlds. A dark, blood-red sun barely hung above the horizon, casting long, twisted shadows over a broken landscape—ruins of cities that once thrived, now nothing but jagged, desolate remains. The wind carried the faint scent of decay, the distant echoes of destruction ringing in the air. What remained of the river lay stagnant, its waters thick with the weight of forgotten lives.

The Seven Sages stood in a broken circle, their figures silhouetted against the barren, oppressive sky. Their robes, once symbols of wisdom and purity, were tattered by the endless storms of Karma Yug. Yet, it wasn't the decay of the land that held their attention—it was the weight of the world pressing down on their shoulders. The air vibrated with tension, a silent battle raging within each of them. In the distance, the people, desperate and broken, looked to them for salvation—not as mere teachers, but as gods.

Rudrayan, the Hammer of Justice, slammed his fist into the earth, the tremors beneath his palm a reflection of the chaos within. His eyes, wild with frustration, locked onto the faces of the others. *"This—this is not what we were meant to be! They—they look at us as if we're gods!"* His words *exploded from his chest like a volcanic eruption, his fists trembling with the force of his emotions. "I never asked for this power. I never wanted them to bow to me, to call me their savior. We only wanted to guide them, not to become their deities!"*

Satyavrat, the Bearer of Truth, clenched his jaw, his chest tight with the heavy burden of their reality. His voice, usually firm and unyielding, wavered in the raw wind. *"The truth... was meant to set them free, not enslave them. We showed them the way, and now they think we are the truth. It's all twisted, corrupted. They look to us as the answer to everything. But we're only human, only Sages! How can they see us as their gods? How could we let this happen?"*

Anirvan, the Flame of Courage, stepped forward, his every movement burning with an inner storm. His voice was laced with raw emotion, his words cracking under the strain of his own internal battle. *"They need us. They depend on us. But they want something more. They want us to save them. To shape the world with a single command, with a single gesture. And I—I can't just turn away. But how can we be their salvation? How can we become their gods?"* His hand shot out, the fury of his frustration palpable, as if he wanted to destroy the very air *around him. "We never wanted this! We wanted to lead them, not rule them!"*

Vidyatman, the Keeper of Knowledge, stood silent, his mind churning with the weight of what had become of their intentions. He could feel the pull of power, like an unseen force threading through the air, wrapping around them. *"They... they don't see us anymore as mere Sages,"* he said *quietly, his words cutting through the tension like a knife. "They see us as the masters of fate itself. They look to us as if we alone hold the keys to salvation. And we—we are powerless to stop it. This is what they want. They see us as gods, and no matter what we say, no matter what we do, it feels like we're becoming them."* His eyes hardened, as if he could already sense the coming storm of consequences.

Karunesh, the Vessel of Mercy, lowered his head, his heart heavy with sorrow. The wind tore at his robes, but it was nothing compared to the gnawing anguish inside. *"How did we let this happen?" His voice broke with the weight of his words. "We came to heal them, to offer mercy and compassion, but now... they expect us to carry their burdens, their pain, their lives on our shoulders. They pray to us, as though we are gods. How can we stand for this? How can we live with this?"* He sank to his knees, his body shaking, not from the wind, but from the weight of their responsibility. *"We never sought power. But now they need us... and it feels like a trap."*

Yuktashakti, the Weaver of Fate, stood apart from the others, her fingers lightly tracing the air as if weaving the strands of destiny. But her movements were slow, deliberate, as if even fate itself could no longer be trusted. *"We cannot change the course of fate, but we've become its architects," she said, her voice steady but heavy with the burden of truth. "The people need us, yes. But they need us as gods. They believe we can shape their lives, bend the world to their will. But we did not come here to rule. We came to guide them through the chaos, to teach them to control their own fate. But now…" She stopped, a bitter laugh escaping her lips. "Now they see us as the very creators of their fate."*

Nirvansh, the Master of Desire, stood at the very edge of their circle, his face an unreadable mask. The winds tousled his hair, but there was something deeper, darker, stirring within him. *"We've failed," he whispered, his voice barely audible. "We fought to master desire, to understand it. But now, I fear it is mastering us. We didn't want to become their gods. We didn't want them to worship us. But now… every whisper, every prayer, every moment of their dependence… it feels like we're drowning in it. And we're letting it happen. We're letting them turn us into gods."*

The Dawn of Unity: Embracing the Sacred Duty

In that profound moment of stillness, the Seven Sages stood together, their hearts heavy with the enormity of what lay ahead, yet filled with a quiet reverence for the path they were about to walk. The weight of their previous doubts, frustrations, and misunderstandings began to melt away, replaced by a deep, shared understanding of their true purpose. They were not chosen to rule, nor to be worshipped. They were chosen to guide, to lead by example, to show others the way through their own actions and choices. The power they had been given was not to be used for control, but to help others unlock their own strength, wisdom, and potential.

Each Sage, in that moment, felt an overwhelming sense of humility and gratitude. They had been entrusted with an immense responsibility, not because they were the greatest or the most powerful, but because they had the willingness to embrace their own flaws and imperfections, and to use those very imperfections to help others find their own path. Their role was not to impose their will, but to help others discover the power within themselves to live with balance, to understand the consequences of their actions, and to live in harmony with the world.

The realization was clear: justice was not about enforcing punishment, but teaching others to live with integrity. Truth was not a weapon to manipulate, but a light to guide those brave enough to seek it. Courage was not about fighting battles for others, but about inspiring them to face their own struggles with strength and resilience. Knowledge was not a treasure to hoard, but a gift to share, to help others unlock their own understanding. Mercy was not about shielding others from suffering, but about teaching them how to endure it, how to find peace within even the most painful moments. Fate was not something they could control, but a path they could help others navigate, showing them how to walk through life with purpose and intention. Desire was not to be suppressed, but to be understood, harnessed for creation and growth, not destruction.

As they stood there, a deep sense of respect for one another filled their hearts. Each Sage, despite their differences, saw the value in the others. They understood that their individual struggles, their imperfections, were what made them whole, what made them the perfect guides for this new era. They were not rivals, not competitors for power, but allies, each contributing their unique strengths to the collective mission. There was no room for ego, no desire for recognition. They were, at that moment, truly united in purpose, knowing that only through unity could they fulfill the great responsibility placed upon them.

The gratitude they felt for being chosen by the supreme Gods was overwhelming. They had not been selected because they were flawless or powerful, but because they had the capacity for self-awareness, humility, and the desire to help others. They felt humbled, knowing that this was not just an honor, but a sacred duty. They were not gods to be worshipped, but servants of a greater cause—servants to the people, to the world, and to the greater design of Karma Yug.

Each Sage, in their heart, silently thanked the supreme Gods for this opportunity, for entrusting them with the rebirth of the world. They felt a deep sense of responsibility, not just for themselves, but for every soul they would guide. And as the realization of their role settled in, they found a profound sense of peace in knowing they were not alone in this mission. They had each other, and they had the unwavering faith of the Gods to carry them through.

With this understanding, they each silently accepted the weight of their roles, knowing that this was their destiny. Their acceptance was not born of pride, but of a deep and sincere commitment to the greater good. Karma Yug was not to be shaped by force, but by wisdom, compassion, and understanding. Together, they would guide humanity, not as gods, but as humble guides— leading with grace, showing others how to rule their own lives through their actions, their karma. In that moment, they all stood united, hearts full of humility, respect, and a deep, unshakable gratitude for the supreme Gods who had chosen them to carry forth this monumental task. They were ready.

Chapter 6

The Rise of the Shadow

The battlefield trembles under the weight of two opposing forces. The ground, cracked and scorched, bears the scars of countless battles fought before this moment. The sky churns with ominous clouds, flashing with streaks of violet and crimson lightning, as if the heavens themselves bear witness to the looming clash. Ash drifts in the air, carried by howling winds that whisper the ghosts of Kalyug's destruction.

The seven sages stand unwavering, their divine energy pulsating like the last beacon of hope. Their robes, flowing like celestial banners, radiate a luminescent glow that pierces through the surrounding gloom. Each of them emanates an aura of power, their eyes reflecting not just determination, but the weight of an entire age resting upon their shoulders.

Across them, Ranjeet stands tall, shrouded in a darkness so thick it seems to drink the light around him. His form is draped in a flowing cloak that shifts like liquid shadow, its edges curling like tendrils of ink against the dim glow of the battlefield. His eyes burn—not with righteousness, but with the fury of a fallen star, their crimson glow pulsing like dying embers refusing to be extinguished. His face, sharp and gaunt, carries the cruel elegance of a fallen deity, his lips curled into a knowing smirk that hints at untold horrors. His skin, a deep ashen hue, bears scars that glisten faintly under the storm-ridden sky—markings of a forgotten past, etched in both pain and defiance.

Behind him, a legion of shadows—souls twisted by his corruption—rise, their hollow eyes flickering with eerie phosphorescence. They are wraiths of greed and ambition, remnants of Kalyug's most desperate, their forms shifting and writhing like a grotesque tide waiting to crash upon the world. The very air around Ranjeet vibrates with an unseen force, a malevolent aura that seems to twist reality itself, bending time and space in silent torment. The battlefield, already ruined, groans under his presence, as though the earth itself recoils from the weight of his existence.

Yet, the weight of such a transformation was immense. Shadows of the past still lingered, whispering doubt into the hearts of men. The remnants of Kalyug had not vanished overnight. Old powers clung to their influence, resisting change with cunning and force. It was in this fragile dawn of a new era that the sages found themselves facing an enemy unlike any before—one who understood the darkest corners of the human soul, who thrived not through war, but through corruption.

A gust of wind sweeps across the ruins of Kalyug, carrying with it the scent of decay and forgotten battles. The distant echoes of wailing souls seem to ride upon the howling gales, whispering secrets buried by time. And then—Yuktashakti freezes.

His pupils dilate, his body rigid as though seized by an unseen force. His breath turns shallow, almost nonexistent, as an eerie chill snakes up his spine. The blood drains from his face, his hands trembling at his sides. A long-forgotten dread, buried deep within the corridors of his mind, erupts to the surface, sending waves of cold sweat cascading down his back. His lips part, but for a moment, no words escape—only silence, thick and suffocating, as recognition strikes him like a bolt of divine lightning.

Yuktashakti (whispering, stunned, voice trembling, barely above a breath): *"This… this cannot be. You were the one… the guiding light, the beacon of hope. They… we… everyone believed in you. I believed in you! You were meant to lead us, to save us, not—"* Her voice cracks, her breath hitching as disbelief crashes into her like a tidal wave. *"Not this. Not the darkness. Not… this betrayal. Tell me, Ranjeet—was it all a lie? Were we nothing more than pawns in your game?"*

The weight of memory collapsed upon her like a mountain. The face before her was no stranger—it was a ghost from a dream she had dared to forget.

Ranjeet smirks, stepping forward, his presence overwhelming, suffocating.

Ranjeet (mocking, arms outstretched, his voice dripping with dark amusement): *"Finally, someone remembers! Ah, the weight of memory—so heavy, so burdensome, isn't it? And yet, here we are, with the past clawing its way back into the light."* His

Each word struck like a whip, not merely mocking her
pain but awakening a deeper fear—that the divine plan
had flaws, that even the chosen could fall.

The other sages exchange glances—Satyavrat's grip
tightens on his staff, Rudrayan's knuckles whiten around
his weapon. What was Yuktashakti saying?

Karunesh, the Vessel of Mercy (calm, yet firm):
"Yuktashakti, what do you mean? Who is he?"

Yuktashakti's voice wavers, her mind racing through
memories the Supreme Gods had sealed away.

Yuktashakti (shaken, voice cracking): *"He... he was meant
to be the first, the harbinger of change. The Supreme Gods did not
merely choose him—they entrusted him with the holiest of missions.
He was to walk among men as both sword and shield, to purge
the corruption that had seeped into every crevice of existence. His
hands were meant to carve a path for Kalki's arrival, to set the
stage for the final cleansing of Kalyug. He was to endure, to resist
temptation, to uphold Dharma even when the world around him
crumbled.*

But he—he turned away. He was sent into Kalyug not just to cleanse it, but to wait—to call upon Kalki when his task was complete. Yet, instead of wielding his divine duty as a weapon of purification, he let the filth of Kalyug consume him. He chose greed over justice, comfort over struggle, luxury over sacrifice. He was seduced by power, by the lure of ruling rather than serving, of being worshipped rather than leading with humility. And now, he stands before us, not as a savior, but as the very darkness he was sworn to destroy!"

Silence.

Deadly. Deafening.

Then—Satyavrat steps forward, his eyes piercing through Ranjeet like an unyielding flame.

Satyavrat (growling): *"Lies. The Supreme Gods would never choose a being of such corruption!"*

Ranjeet chuckles—a dark, guttural sound laced with mockery.

Ranjeet (low, taunting): *"Oh, but they did. You see, my dear sages, the Gods had faith in me. They thought I would cleanse this world of its filth, that I would wield divine fire and burn Kalyug's sins to ash. And then what? Hand it over to Kalki like a dutiful servant? Accept my role as nothing more than a tool, a mere instrument for a fate someone else dictated?"*

His eyes blaze with fury, his voice growing sharper, laced with scorn. *"They expected me to clean Kalyug, to rid it of its filth and then step aside? Really? When I have the strength, the capability, the power to rule? To shape the world in my own image? They thought I would bow after witnessing the limitless indulgence, the pleasures, the obedience of men who crave dominion over freedom? No, sages. I was not cast aside—I chose my own path!"*

His voice drops, thick with venom.

Ranjeet (sinister, eyes narrowing): *"But when I came to this world… oh, how magnificent it was. The power. The pleasures. The way men bowed before me, offering their loyalty for a mere taste of dominance. Why should I destroy it when I could rule it?"*

His laughter echoes like thunder.

Vidyatman, the Keeper of Knowledge (shaking his head, horrified): *"You turned away from Dharma. You were given the highest honor, and yet… you embraced sin."*

Ranjeet's grin fades, his jaw tightening.

Ranjeet (furious, voice rising): *"SIN?! You dare call it sin?! The Gods sent me to purge this world, and yet, when I chose my own path, they abandoned me! They erased me from history, as if I never existed! Tell me, who speaks of me now? Who remembers my name in prayers, in songs, in scriptures? NO ONE! I was their chosen warrior, their first, and yet they cast me into oblivion the moment I defied their will!"*

His voice trembles—not just with rage, but with something deeper… betrayal.

Ranjeet (dark, sneering): *"Tell me, O Wise Ones, what is the greater crime? That I embraced the truth of this world, or that your*

Gods discarded their own chosen warrior the moment he refused to be their puppet? You tell me—who knows me?!"

Rudrayan, the Hammer of Justice (thundering, unwavering): *"ENOUGH!"*

A silence fell—not of peace, but of dread. The sages did not merely stand against darkness; they stood against betrayal, against a future that mirrored the sins of the past.

His voice cuts through the night like divine judgment. He steps forward, towering over Ranjeet, his presence unshaken.

Rudrayan (fierce, burning with righteous wrath): *"You were never abandoned, Ranjeet. You abandoned yourself! The Gods do not dictate our choices—they grant us the wisdom to choose. And you chose corruption. You chose greed. You chose to spit upon the very purpose of your existence!"*

Ranjeet's nostrils flare. His fingers twitch. The shadows around him writhe like serpents.

Ranjeet (dangerous, voice dripping with menace): *"And yet, here I stand, more powerful than any of you! The Gods may have chosen you to build Karma Yug, but I… I will burn it to the ground."*

He raises his hand—a wave of darkness surges forward, consuming everything in its path.

The sages brace themselves, their divine energy colliding with the abyss. The ground trembles. The sky darkens. The battle of fate begins.

With their purpose crystallized, the seven sages had stepped forth into the dawn of Karma Yug, hearts united in humility and gratitude. They were not rulers, nor divine saviors, but guides entrusted with the sacred task of leading humanity through wisdom and action. Their vision was clear—to reshape a world corrupted by greed and blind ambition, to plant the seeds of a future where karma alone would dictate fate.

Yet, the weight of such a transformation was immense. Shadows of the past still lingered, whispering doubt into the hearts of men. The remnants of Kalyug had not vanished overnight. Old powers clung to their influence, resisting change with cunning and force. It was in this fragile dawn of a new era that the sages found themselves facing an enemy unlike any before—one who understood the darkest corners of the human soul, who thrived not through war, but through corruption.

And so, as they took their first steps into this uncharted future, an unsettling truth loomed—change was never unchallenged.

The great hall trembled, its ancient stone pillars groaning under the weight of an unseen force. Shadows danced wildly across the towering walls as torches flickered in the thick, suffocating air. The seven sages stood in the center, their robes whispering against the marble floor, their faces set like stone. Across from them, looming like an unshakable monolith, stood Ranjeet.

The self-made emperor of greed leaned lazily against his golden staff, its serpent-shaped head gleaming under the wavering torchlight. His smirk was carved with unshaken arrogance, his eyes glinting like embers in the half-darkness. The air around him was heavy, thick with the stench of power unchecked. He exuded the confidence of a man who had never been denied, never been humbled. The very walls of the chamber seemed to bow under the weight of his presence, as if the very foundations of Karma Yug shuddered at his defiance.

"So this is the grand council of the so-called architects of a new age?" Ranjeet's voice dripped with mockery, his smirk widening as he let his gaze sweep over them. "I expected wisdom, but all I see are dreamers clinging to illusions. Karma Yug? What a delightful farce! We waited for Satya Yug, for gods to descend and cleanse this world, but instead, we got you?" He let out a sharp, derisive laugh. "Tell me, sages, what exactly do you think you can do for us? Preach some hollow wisdom? Deliver empty promises? Or will you merely watch as the world tramples your ideals into the dust?" He stepped forward, eyes gleaming with venom. "Power does not reward the virtuous; it bows to the ruthless. And I, dear sages, am the only god this era will ever need.""

Rudrayan stepped forward, his stance unshaken, his presence exuding a quiet authority. The dim torchlight cast flickering shadows across his serene face, but his voice carried no anger, only unwavering resolve. *"Power without righteousness is a sword wielded by the blind. Strength without wisdom is chaos. You, Ranjeet, are not a ruler—you are a man who has mistaken his chains for a throne. You cling to an era that has already crumbled, refusing to see the new dawn rising before you."* He paused, his calm gaze holding Ranjeet's with steady patience. *"We are not here to rule, nor to demand submission. We are here to remind humanity of its own strength, its own destiny. Karma Yug does not ask for obedience—it asks for understanding, for action born from truth rather than fear."*

Ranjeet chuckled, slow and deliberate, his lips curling into a sneer. *"Is that what you believe? That Kalyug is truly dead? That your grand words and pious wisdom have wiped away the filth of this world?"* His eyes gleamed with dangerous amusement. *"Fools. Kalyug never dies—it only changes its skin. And I? I am its chosen voice. The gods abandoned this world, and in their absence, I ruled. You come here preaching about a new dawn, but you are nothing more than lost men chasing a mirage. What can you possibly offer that the world hasn't already rejected?"* He leaned in slightly, his tone dripping with mockery. *"Hope? Justice? A fair world? Hah! People don't crave fairness, they crave survival. And survival, dear sages, belongs to the cunning, to those who wield true power. So tell me—what makes you think you can stand against me?"*

Vidyatman narrowed his gaze, his voice steady as a mountain, unshaken by Ranjeet's venom. *"You poison minds with greed, twist desires into chains, and call it leadership. But power built on fear is an illusion, Ranjeet. It crumbles the moment the fear fades. Your empire was not forged in strength—it was carved from the helplessness of those you exploit. And yet, you stand here, believing yourself invincible."*

"And they willingly bowed," Ranjeet countered, his voice a serpent's whisper, laced with venomous amusement. "The weak crave guidance, yes—but they also crave chains. They seek someone to command, someone to blame, someone to worship. If not me, then another would have taken my place. And you, sages, with your grand delusions of Karma Yug—do you truly believe you are any different?" He sneered, his eyes narrowing. "You do not offer freedom. You offer another leash, wrapped in the sweet lie of 'destiny.'"

Nirvansh's voice was steady, carrying no malice, only an unshakable truth. "Ranjeet, leadership is not measured by how many bow before you, but by how many rise because of you. You claim power, yet all you have built is fear. You twist desires into shackles, turn ambition into servitude, and call it leadership. But true strength does not control—it liberates. And you, for all your might, are still a prisoner of your own greed."

Ranjeet's smirk deepened, his voice thick with derision. "And yet, you stand here, clutching your fragile dream of Karma Yug, a world ruled by merit? What a pathetic fantasy! Do you truly think the masses crave justice? No, sages, they crave comfort. They are spineless creatures, eager to trade their morals for a warm meal, their values for the illusion of security. They do not want truth, they want an easy lie. And you—you're nothing but peddlers of hope in a world that has long since abandoned it."

Anirvan exhaled sharply, loosening his clenched fists as he met Ranjeet's sneering gaze. His voice, though firm, carried the patience of a teacher addressing a stubborn student. "Then we shall remind them that their strength was never lost, only buried beneath fear and deception. We shall not burn *illusions with fire, but dissolve them with truth. We are not here to destroy, Ranjeet—we are here to awaken."*

Ranjeet sighed, feigning disappointment. *"Ah, the idealist. Tell me, what happens when the fire consumes the very ones you wish to protect? Will you still believe in this 'justice' when the people you cherish turn against you?"* He gestured towards the city beyond the hall, where his influence seeped through every alley and every mind.

Karunesh's voice carried the warmth of a mother consoling her lost child. *"Ranjeet, my heart aches for you and for all who have been led astray. You have wrapped them in fear, taught them to see the world through its dark veil. But fear is not the truth—it is merely a shadow, and all shadows fade when light finds them. We are not here to take anything from you, not to condemn, but to show another way. No shadow lasts forever, my child, and neither will this."*

Even in the face of malevolence, his voice held the softness of spring after a cruel winter. He did not speak to the tyrant—he spoke to the boy buried deep within the monster.

Ranjeet's laughter roared through the hall, thick with scorn. *"Oh, how noble! The wise sages, the shepherds of the lost, the saviors of a world too foolish to save itself! Tell me, do you truly believe your wisdom holds weight against power? That your sermons can silence the hunger of greed?"* He sneered, eyes gleaming with derision. *"You come here, draped in righteousness, speaking of karma and justice as if they are shields against the inevitable. But I ask you, sages—what happens when men spit on your wisdom? When they trade your so-called 'truth' for comfort and servitude?*

What will you do when they choose me over you?" He spread his arms wide, his grin cutting like a blade. *"Then come, sages of Karma Yug. Prove to me that your world is stronger than mine. Show me that your fire can outshine my darkness!"*

The sages exchanged glances, a silent acknowledgment passing between them. This was no mere clash of words or steel—this was a war of ideologies, a battle for the very essence of humanity's future. And they would not falter.

The sages are challenged not just as individuals but as a collective force. The storm above rumbles like an omen, and the air is thick with tension. Ranjeet, cunning as ever, understands that brute force will not break them. Instead, he plays a different game—the game of temptation. A slow smirk spreads across his face as he steps forward, the flickering torches casting long shadows behind him. He approaches each sage, his voice dripping with honeyed persuasion, offering them something so irresistibly perfect that even the strongest might waver. His words slither through the air, wrapping around the sages like a serpent tightening its coil, testing their resolve, their unity, and the very foundation of their beliefs.

Ranjeet turns first to Rudrayan – The Hammer of Justice. *"Why fight corruption when you can rule over it?"* he taunts. *"With my wealth and power, you could build an empire of justice. No more waiting for justice—you will decide who lives and who dies."* *The vision is intoxicating, a world where no crime goes unpunished, where justice is swift and absolute. But Rudrayan sees through the illusion. "Justice that bows to power is not justice," he thunders, his voice slicing through the air. He turns away, rejecting the offer.*

Next, Ranjeet faces Satyavrat – The Bearer of Truth. He offers him dominion over all forms of communication. *"No more lies, no more deception," Ranjeet whispers. "Every word spoken, every story written, every truth told—it will all be under your control." For a moment, Satyavrat imagines a world free from manipulation, where only truth prevails. But then he shakes his head. "A truth that fears challenge is no truth at all," he declares, stepping back.*

Ranjeet moves on to Anirvan – The Flame of Courage. *"Fear is your enemy, is it not?" he says smoothly. "What if I could erase it entirely? Imagine a world where no warrior hesitates, where no battle is lost to doubt. I can give you that." Anirvan feels the weight of the offer, the promise of a fearless world. But then he smiles, his fire undiminished. "Courage is not the absence of fear, but the strength to face it," he replies, dismissing Ranjeet's words.*

Turning to Vidyatman – The Keeper of Knowledge, Ranjeet unveils a golden scroll, shimmering with ethereal light. *"Every lost scripture, every secret of the cosmos, every answer you have ever sought—it is yours. No more searching, no more questioning. Only complete wisdom." Vidyatman's hands tremble slightly, for he has spent lifetimes in pursuit of knowledge. But then, he closes his eyes and lets out a breath. "Wisdom must be earned, not gifted," he says, turning away.*

With a smirk, Ranjeet approaches Karunesh – The Vessel of Mercy. *"End all suffering," he offers. "One word, and I will erase every pain, every sorrow. You will become the true savior of mankind." Karunesh's heart aches at the thought, at the possibility of a world without suffering. But then he sees the flaw. "Compassion is not eliminating suffering; it is guiding one through it," he says softly. His refusal is gentle, yet firm.*

To Yuktashakti – The Weaver of Fate, Ranjeet offers the grandest temptation of all—control over destiny itself. *"No more uncertainty, no more chaos. You can weave the perfect future for all. Imagine the peace, the perfection." Yuktashakti gazes at the swirling strands of fate, the infinite possibilities before her. But she knows the cost. "Destiny is not to be controlled, but understood," she states, stepping back.*

Finally, Ranjeet turns to Nirvansh – The Master of Desire. His voice is almost reverent as he speaks. *"You have spent your existence mastering desire, taming its flames. But what if I could free you entirely? No more struggle, no more longing. Pure, eternal peace. Isn't that what you seek?" Nirvansh smiles, for he has already learned his lesson. "Desire is not the enemy—it is the fire that fuels life. True mastery is not in escaping it, but in embracing it with balance."*

One by one, the sages deny what no mortal could refuse. The air thickens with tension as each rejection lands like a hammer blow on Ranjeet's confidence. He watches, his smirk faltering, as his greatest trick unravels before his eyes. These were not mere refusals; they were declarations—of will, of wisdom, of the unbreakable force that bound the sages together.

Ranjeet clenches his fists, his nails digging deep into his palms, drawing tiny crescents of blood. *"You fools!*

You blind, delusional fools! Do you not see? This world is built on bargains! Everything—everything—has a price!" His voice rises, raw and laced with disbelief. His carefully crafted facade of arrogance crumbles into naked frustration. *"Why choose the hard path when perfection is within reach? Why grovel in the dirt when you could rule from the heavens? Why suffer like beggars when I offer you the throne?"* His chest heaves with ragged breaths, his fury tangible in the suffocating air around them.

His fury was a storm—but not the kind that comes from power. It was the cry of a man who had bet everything on darkness and found no warmth in its embrace.

Rudrayan steps forward, his presence like an unyielding mountain. *"Because power without struggle is an illusion. And we do not barter with illusions."*

Satyavrat's voice follows, steady as the flow of time itself. *"Truth that is gifted is no truth at all. It is a leash disguised as freedom."*

Anirvan's fiery gaze meets Ranjeet's. *"Courage is tested in the face of fear, not in its absence. You offer emptiness, not strength."*

Vidyatman shakes his head, the wisdom of ages glinting in his eyes. *"Knowledge without effort is not knowledge. It is a cage."*

Karunesh's voice is barely above a whisper, yet it carries the weight of boundless compassion. *"Suffering is not the enemy. It is the teacher."*

Yuktashakti speaks next, weaving fate itself in her words. *"Control is an illusion. True destiny lies in understanding, not domination."*

And finally, Nirvansh, the master of desire, the one who knew its depths and its fire, steps forward. His smile is calm, unwavering. *"Desire is not to be conquered. It is to be balanced. Your temptations are chains, not gifts."*

A silence follows—heavy, absolute. Ranjeet takes a step back. Then another. The weight of his failure crashes down upon him. For the first time, he sees it—not just the sages before him, but the truth they embody. Karma Yug cannot be bought. It cannot be manipulated. It must be earned.

With a final glare, he vanishes into the shadows, his presence dissipating like a fading storm. Yet, his rage lingers in the air, thick and venomous, a testament to the battle he lost not through might, but through will. The sages stand unmoved, their unity an unbreakable fortress against deceit. A knowing silence passes between them, a shared understanding that words cannot capture. Then, one by one, they exchange glances—soft smiles of reassurance, eyes gleaming with the quiet confidence of those who have faced the storm and emerged unshaken.

Rudrayan clasps Anirvan's shoulder, a firm acknowledgment of their shared strength. Satyavrat exhales, his gaze sweeping over his companions with unspoken gratitude. Karunesh bows his head slightly, the warmth of his compassion radiating in his serene smile.

Yuktashakti and Nirvansh share a brief but telling look—one of deep respect, of unwavering resolve. Vidyatman, ever the seeker, watches them all, knowing that wisdom is not in mere knowledge, but in the unity they now embodied.

As the echoes of Ranjeet's shattered scheme fade into the wind, the sages turn to one another—not as individuals, but as a collective force, bound by purpose, standing together at the dawn of a world they must now shape anew.

Yet, even as they stood united, a shadow loomed over their newfound resolve. The world was not ready to surrender to the order of Karma Yug so easily. Ranjeet's defeat had only scattered the embers of his corruption, not extinguished them. In the alleys of forgotten cities and the chambers of power, whispers of defiance began to rise. The old ways did not crumble overnight, and those who had thrived in the chaos of Kalyug would not yield without resistance.

Doubt crept into the hearts of the sages. Could they truly break the cycle of Kalyug, or were they merely delaying the inevitable? Rudrayan's mind wrestled with the echoes of past ages—had not each yuga before this succumbed to its own destruction? What made Karma Yug any different? His hands clenched at his sides, the weight of responsibility pressing down like an unseen force. Satyavrat, the bearer of truth, found himself questioning whether men could ever willingly choose righteousness over desire. Could truth stand firm in a world so accustomed to deceit?

Anirvan clenched his fists, frustrated by the unseen enemy—the inertia of human nature itself. His mind flashed with images of warriors who had fallen to greed, to fear, to doubt. Could courage alone carve a new path? Even Nirvansh, master of restraint, felt the silent fear of an age that might reject the path laid before it. He had spent lifetimes mastering desire, yet he questioned whether men would ever seek balance on their own, or whether they would always be bound by their cravings.

A whisper of unease curled through the group, unspoken but tangible. Were they fighting a battle already lost?

Vidyatman's wisdom wavered for the first time, as he pondered the enormity of their task. *"Have we misjudged the world's readiness? Have we misjudged ourselves?" he murmured. Yuktashakti, who had always woven fate's threads with certainty, now saw strands unravel before her eyes. Even Karunesh, the ever-compassionate, felt the weight of sorrow for those who clung to their suffering, unwilling to step into the light.*

Was Karma Yug destined to fail before it had even begun?

Rudrayan took a step forward, his presence commanding yet devoid of arrogance. He had chosen to take the lead, to ensure that those who listened could begin to believe in change for the better. With a steady breath, he met Ranjeet's gaze and spoke, his voice measured but resolute. *"Justice may have shattered Ranjeet, but what of those who still cling to his vision?"* His words carried no malice, only the weight of concern.

Ranjeet, weakened but still defiant, sneered. *"You think you have won? You are nothing but blind idealists, clinging to illusions of order while the world laughs at your naïveté. Look around you—what do you see? Men who crave justice? No, sages. Men who crave power, survival, wealth. They will not rise for your ideals. They will trample them. Your so-called Karma Yug is a delusion, a fleeting mirage that will be crushed beneath the weight of reality. And you? You will watch it crumble, powerless to stop it.""*

Satyavrat stepped forward, his expression calm, his voice steady yet humble. *"We do not seek to force anything, Ranjeet. Change cannot be imposed—it must be embraced. We only strive to restore balance where chaos has reigned for too long."*

Anirvan inhaled deeply, his earlier frustration melting into quiet understanding. For a fleeting moment, he wondered—was Ranjeet right? Could the darkness within men never truly be vanquished? The thought passed, but it left a lingering shadow in his mind. He exhaled slowly, grounding himself in the belief that the struggle itself was worth it. *"You are not our enemy, Ranjeet. Not truly. The real battle is not against men, but against the darkness that lingers in all of us. Even in us. But that does not mean we surrender to it.""*

Nirvansh's gaze softened, his tone almost soothing. *"You see us as oppressors because change is terrifying. We understand. But Karma Yug is not a chain—it is a choice. One that leads away from suffering, if only one dares to walk it."*

Karunesh took a step closer, his voice filled with gentle warmth. *"You have spent your life seeking power, Ranjeet. But power alone has never saved a soul. What if, for once, you sought something greater than control? What if you sought peace?"*

Yuktashakti nodded, his words carrying the patience of one who understood the tides of time. *"Even the strongest currents cannot fight the ocean. You, too, are part of this change. And like all of us, you have a choice—to resist or to grow."*

Vidyatman, who had listened in silence, finally spoke, but there was a rare hesitation in his voice. He was the keeper of knowledge, yet even he could not predict the future of Karma Yug. Was it hubris to believe they could shape the world? Had history not proven time and again that the cycle would repeat? He closed his eyes for a moment, seeking clarity, before finally saying, *"This is the true trial of Karma Yug. Not in its inception, but in its survival. Philosophy alone will not sustain it; only action aligned with dharma will. But what is dharma in a world still drenched in the sins of the past? That is the question we all must answer. And we must be prepared for the world to challenge that answer every step of the way.""*

A gust of wind swept across the barren land, carrying the last remnants of Ranjeet's presence into the void. In its wake, uncertainty remained. The sages had vanquished a tyrant, but the battle for Karma Yug had only begun.

Yet, just as doubt began to take root, a soft glow emerged on the distant horizon. A group of weary travelers approached, their eyes filled with reverence, their hands folded in gratitude.

A single flame can resist a thousand shadows—and sometimes, the light comes not from those who preach, but from those who have only just begun to believe.

"You have given us hope," an elder among them spoke, his voice trembling with both weariness and newfound belief. "For the first time, we see a path beyond the darkness of Kalyug. We had long thought righteousness was a relic of the past, buried beneath the weight of corruption. But today, we see that light can still rise, that justice is not lost, and that perhaps, we too can be part of this change."

The sages exchanged glances, the weight of their doubts lifting ever so slightly. The travelers before them were not rulers or warriors, not men of great influence or wealth. They were the ordinary souls of the world—farmers, artisans, wanderers—those who had suffered the most under the decay of Kalyug. And yet, in their eyes burned a quiet determination, a willingness to embrace something new. Perhaps the world was not entirely lost. Perhaps, amidst the resistance and uncertainty, there were still hearts willing to embrace the new dawn.

Rudrayan straightened his stance, his expression firm yet kind. He took a slow step forward, his eyes meeting those of the weary travelers, then turning back to his fellow sages. *"Then we shall not waver,"* he declared, his voice resolute but gentle. *"For if even a single soul dares to believe in change, then Karma Yug is not a dream—it is a reality waiting to be built. We have not come to dictate its course, but to guide those willing to walk its path. And as long as there is one heart willing to embrace the light, we shall stand unwavering in our purpose."*

Anirvan's grip loosened, his fire tempered with renewed purpose. Satyavrat, Karunesh, Yuktashakti, Nirvansh, and Vidyatman each felt it—the fragile but undeniable proof that their mission was not in vain.

They had stood firm against Ranjeet, but now, as they faced the uncertainty of their path, doubt crept into their hearts. Had they truly broken the cycle, or had they merely delayed its inevitable return?

Rudrayan's mind wrestled with the echoes of past ages— had not each yuga before this succumbed to its own destruction? What made Karma Yug any different? His hands clenched at his sides, the weight of responsibility pressing down like an unseen force. Satyavrat, the bearer of truth, found himself questioning whether men could ever willingly choose righteousness over desire. Could truth stand firm in a world so accustomed to deceit?

Anirvan clenched his fists, frustrated by the unseen enemy—the inertia of human nature itself. His mind flashed with images of warriors who had fallen to greed, to fear, to doubt. Could courage alone carve a new path? Even Nirvansh, master of restraint, felt the silent fear of an age that might reject the path laid before it. He had spent lifetimes mastering desire, yet he questioned whether men would ever seek balance on their own, or whether they would always be bound by their cravings.

But hesitation was a luxury they could not afford. A gust of wind swirled through the ruins, as if the world itself demanded their decision.

The embers of Kalyug had not yet died, but neither had the light of Karma Yug. In the ashes of the old world, a flicker of hope remained—delicate yet unyielding, like the first ray of dawn piercing through the remnants of a long, dark night. It was not the end, but the beginning of a battle worth fighting, a path worth treading, and a future still waiting to be written.

A distant rumble of thunder echoed through the sky, as if the gods themselves watched in silent anticipation. The sages stood on the precipice of history, their resolve unshaken, their purpose clear. This was no longer just an era—they were its architects. And the world would remember.

In that silence, something eternal was written—not in stone, but in soul. Karma Yug was no longer just an age. It was a vow, echoing not from the heavens, but from the hearts of the brave.

And so they stood, not as legends, but as lanterns in the gathering dark.

Their robes bore the dust of battles fought in silence, their eyes the weight of choices etched into time.

They had not vanquished evil—they had simply chosen to face it, again and again, with open hearts.

Karma Yug was not born from victory, but from resistance.

Not from certainty, but from the willingness to walk the uncertain road with truth as their only compass.

They had not come to end darkness—but to light one spark within it.

And that spark, though small, could become a sun—

If only enough hearts chose to tend its flame.

The sages did not walk away in triumph. They walked away in silence.

Not because they had nothing left to say, but because the world finally had something to hear.

And the gods, who had once ruled in noise and fire, now watched in stillness—

For the world was no longer theirs to command, but theirs to witness.

The battlefield was not merely a place—it was a memory carved into the land. Each scorched stone whispered of past regrets, each gust of wind carried remnants of screams long faded. The air shimmered not with heat, but with unresolved karma, as though the very elements remembered the crimes of Kalyug.

Above them, the sky had fractured into bruised purple and bloodred veins, pulsing like the wrath of forgotten deities. The clouds roared, not with thunder, but with the cries of the past demanding to be heard.

Ranjeet's cloak billowed like living darkness, its movements too deliberate, too sentient. It was as though the shadows around him fed on despair, coiling tighter with every breath he took. Every word he spoke felt like it stained the earth beneath him.

Yuktashakti's vision blurred—not from fear, but from the heartbreak of recognition. This was not just an enemy. This was the echo of a broken promise, the shadow of what could have been. Her divine presence flickered, not from weakness, but from sorrow. The betrayal had not just cracked the sky—it had cracked something within her.

The other sages, though pillars of resolve, felt it too. Karunesh closed his eyes briefly, and in that moment, he saw not Ranjeet the villain, but Ranjeet the child once chosen, once believed in. Satyavrat's breath caught in his throat—truths hidden even from themselves began to surface. Perhaps they had all failed him in ways never spoken.

A sudden wind picked up, stirring the ashes into swirling vortexes. The torches lining the ruins flickered violently, casting chaotic shadows that danced like demons set free. The world seemed to hold its breath—not in anticipation of war, but in mourning for what had already been lost.

Ranjeet stepped forward again, and his voice softened— not in kindness, but in cruelty. *'You stood with me once,'* he said, gaze fixed on Yuktashakti. *'And I would have stood with you. But you all chose duty over love, prophecy over kin. So I forged my truth. Alone.'*

The silence that followed was not empty. It was full— of questions, regrets, echoes. The sages did not answer immediately. Because in their hearts, they knew—they had seen the signs. But in their righteousness, they had looked away.

A low, tremulous light began to emerge from the earth around them—not fire, but something older. Ancient carvings etched into the very ground began to glow, responding not to violence, but to the weight of truth. The battlefield had become a sanctum—not for gods, but for decisions that would echo into eternity.

Rudrayan turned slowly, taking in the cracked stones, the flickering sky, the despair etched into every surface—and still, he stood. For the world needed not saviors, but witnesses—those who would choose light even when surrounded by darkness.

Far above the battlefield, in a time before time, a golden hall shimmered in the eternal plane.

Here, in a sanctum untouched by decay or desire, the Supreme Trinity once gathered—Brahma, Vishnu, and Shiva—bathed in divine light that needed no sun.

A question had arisen that none could answer alone: Who would walk the dying earth and prepare it for its rebirth?

It was then that they turned to the one soul who had once held balance within his heart—a being forged in fire, tempered in knowledge, and destined for sacrifice.

He was not born of pride, but of promise. Ranjeet.

Vishnu spoke first, his voice like rivers flowing across galaxies. *He shall go as the harbinger. Let him cleanse, let him guide, and when the time comes—let him call forth Kalki.'*

Shiva's eyes remained closed, but his third eye flickered. *'Power corrupts those who have not suffered. Let him walk among mortals, let him be tested by fire, lest he forgets who he is.'*

Brahma hesitated, his breath stirring the scrolls of destiny. *'Then we shall not watch. If free will is to rise, it must do so without our interference.'*

And so, Ranjeet was sent—not as a ruler, but as a bridge. Not to dominate, but to prepare.

But no divine eye foresaw what desire would do when left to wander alone in a world still bleeding from its wounds.

Later that night, beneath a canopy of fractured stars, the sages gathered in silence.

The fire between them crackled softly, its light flickering over faces still shadowed with doubt.

They had won—but what had they truly overcome? Was it Ranjeet, or their own illusion of invincibility?

Vidyatman spoke first, his voice low. *We always believed knowledge would save us. But today I learned—understanding comes from loss too.'*

Yuktashakti nodded slowly, tracing invisible threads through the night air. *'Fate has no favorites. It only tests.'*

Karunesh sighed. *'I offered him compassion, but what he needed was time. Perhaps we sent him too soon into a world too broken.'*

Satyavrat's voice cut through the flickering silence. *'There are no perfect warriors. Only those who do not stop walking.'*

And Rudrayan, staring into the flames, whispered, *'Then let us walk. Not as gods, but as those willing to bleed for the light.'*

At dawn, as the storm clouds broke, a new procession appeared—not of armies or kings, but of barefoot pilgrims.

Farmers, potters, children, widows—those left behind by every age that had come before—walked toward the ashes of the battlefield.

They brought no gold, no offerings, only questions... and hope.

An elder approached Rudrayan, his voice shaking. *'Is it true… that this world will no longer be ruled by fear?'*

Rudrayan bent to meet his gaze. *'Not by fear. By action.'*

A young girl tugged at Yuktashakti's robe, her eyes wide. *'Can I choose my future now?'*

Yuktashakti smiled. *'You always could. Now the world will honor that choice.'*

And slowly, the sages knelt—not to be worshipped, but to bless the soil where change had begun.

It was not the end of the war. But it was the beginning of a world where even the smallest voice might rise.

Far above the mortal plane, where silence holds dominion and time breathes slower, the Supreme Trinity watched.

Brahma stood by the Cosmic Scroll, his fingers hovering but unmoving, for he knew this story was no longer his to write.

Vishnu, the Preserver, watched with eyes not of judgment, but of wonder—at the fragility, the fire, and the beauty of mortal will.

And Shiva, the silent storm, sat in stillness, a single tear trailing down the arc of his cheek—not from sorrow, but from surrender.

Shiva (whispering): *They chose... despite the pain, despite the past. They chose light.'*

Vishnu (softly): *Without command. Without miracles. They remembered who they were meant to be.'*

Brahma (resolute): *Then let no god interrupt. Let no divine hand steer. The age of karma belongs to them now.'*

The gods bowed their heads—not in grief, but in reverence. And for the first time in countless eons, the heavens held silence... not as absence, but as respect.

As the sages turned from the battlefield, their silhouettes stretched across the land like eternal vows carved in light.

They walked not toward a temple, nor a throne, but toward the banks of the Ganga—where the waters still remembered every yuga, every fall, every rise.

The river flowed gently, unbothered by empires, untouched by pride. It had carried gods and corpses alike. It had never stopped.

Yuktashakti bent to touch the water, her fingers trembling. *'It remembers,'* she said.

Karunesh smiled, the morning light catching his eyes. *'And it forgives.'*

Rudrayan stepped in silently, the ripples catching his reflection. For a moment, he did not see a sage—but a man, weary, changed, but not broken.

Above them, the first rays of the sun stretched across the horizon, golden and warm. A single bird cried in the distance—not as warning, but as welcome.

The wind shifted, gentle and fragrant. The earth breathed.

And in that breath, the world did not just turn—it awoke.

But hesitation was a luxury they could not afford. A gust of wind swirled through the ruins, as if the world itself demanded their decision.

The embers of Kalyug had not yet died, but neither had the light of Karma Yug. In the ashes of the old world, a flicker of hope remained—delicate yet unyielding, like the first ray of dawn piercing through the remnants of a long, dark night. It was not the end, but the beginning of a battle worth fighting, a path worth treading, and a future still waiting to be written.

A distant rumble of thunder echoed through the sky, as if the gods themselves watched in silent anticipation. The sages stood on the precipice of history, their resolve unshaken, their purpose clear. This was no longer just an era—they were its architects. And the world would remember.

Epilogue

When Silence Becomes Sacred

If you've come this far, perhaps something inside you has changed.

Not loudly. Not suddenly.

But like a slow tide washing over the shore of your soul.

This was never a journey of answers.

It was a walk through silence.

A quiet unfolding of truths that don't roar—but breathe.

We began with gods.

With thunder in the sky, miracles in every breath, and a world where the divine was visible, audible, unshakable.

But somewhere along the way,

they stepped back.

Not in anger,

but in knowing.

They left behind not a map, but a mirror.

And in that mirror, we saw ourselves—flawed, faithful, frightened… but still standing.

This book was never about mythology.

It was about the spaces between the stories.

The moments after the last hymn was sung,

when the lamp flickered alone in the temple wind,

when the devotee stayed—despite no voice answering back.

It is about the sages who stayed after the light faded.

The queens who remembered when others forgot.

The seekers who chose to believe, not because of miracles—but in spite of their absence.

We are not waiting for the gods to return.

We are learning how to live in their silence.

How to carry the divine in our breath,

not on thrones.

How to walk not behind them,

but beside their memory.

And maybe, just maybe—

this silence was never their absence.

Maybe it was their final teaching.

To show us that the sacred has always been within us,

quietly waiting

to be heard.

To you, dear reader—

Thank you for listening.

Thank you for walking this path with me.

Thank you for trusting the silence.

And if someday, the world grows quiet again—

I hope you will know,

you were never alone in it.

With reverence and love,

Parul Mathur